REUNION

REUNION

Dan Foley

A
Grinning Skull Press
Publication

DEDICATION

This book is for Ben Hodgson, high school guidance counselor and basketball coach who saw the potential in me and always celebrated my successes.

CONTENTS

Prologue

What a great day to be alive, Sean McCauley thought as he leaned his head against the window and watched the towns roll by. Sean had gotten on the train in St. Albans, Vermont, and planned to get off in Poquonock. The name was supposed to mean *Land of Good Fortune.* What he didn't know yet was that at least one of the native old timers swore it meant *Place of Slaughter* or *Place of Death.*

Let's just hope it's lucky for me, Sean thought as the train approached Poquonock. He had a dollar in his wallet and a head full of optimism, but that would only take him so far. What he needed was a job. Nothing permanent, just something to put enough in his pocket to bankroll another few weeks of traveling as he continued on his quest to visit every state in the good old U.S.A. After his few weeks here, he planned on visiting New Hampshire and Maine. Then he would start south.

About a mile before the Poquonock station, a steel trestle

carried the train over a crystal clear river that was exactly what he needed—a place to take a quick bath to wash the travel dust off before he went in search of work.

When the train stopped, Sean got off carrying everything he owned—other than the clothes on his back—in a small, well-worn, cardboard suitcase. It contained a toothbrush, toothpaste, a spare shirt and pair of pants, a razor, and a bar of soap. What else would a traveling man need? So, suitcase in hand, he started back down the tracks toward the trestle and the river he had seen from the train.

When he got to the trestle, he looked down at the river and was happy to see it was as clean and clear as it had appeared to be in the few seconds he had glimpsed it from the train. There didn't appear to be a way to get to the river from where he was other than to take a chance on sliding the thirty feet or so down the embankment to the water below.

"Here goes nothing," he said to himself and stepped onto the loose stones and cinders on the embankment. Once he started, there was no turning back. He slid down with both feet spread apart, waving his arms for balance. If he hadn't been as coordinated as he was, he never would have made it without falling. He built up enough speed on the way down that he had to take several running steps when he reached the bottom to keep from tumbling ass-over-teakettle into the bushes that lined the riverbank.

When he came to a stop and looked back up the embankment, he thought, *Maybe this* is *the Land of Good Fortune. I'm lucky I didn't break my fool neck sliding down here.*

Sean found a path that ran along the river's bank and decided he'd follow it. On his return trip he'd try to find an easier way back up to the tracks, but right now he needed a bath. The river was crystal clear, but too shallow and open here. In less than a hundred yards he found the ideal spot where the bottom dropped away to form a deeper pool and leaves from the trees shielded it from the trestle. *Perfect,* he thought as he dug out his soap. Then he took off his boots, stripped off his clothes, folded them, and placed them on the suitcase.

When he stepped into the river, he was shocked by how cold it was. Goose flesh popped out over his entire body, and he almost climbed back out. There was no way he'd find work looking like he did, so he steeled himself, took the plunge, and dove into the pool. The water wasn't any warmer there, but once he got used to it, the chill wasn't so bad. He was happy to find out it only came up to his armpits and the bottom was filled with gravel, not mud. *I'm going to like this place,* he thought as he worked his soap into a lather.

Sean had just finished washing his body and was working the soap into his hair when the river erupted in a shower of soap and water. He barely had time to react before something grabbed him and wrapped itself around him. Whatever it was, it was incredibly strong. He got the impression of a large, snake-like body before claws raked his chest and back in an explosion of pain. Blood filled the water. A reptilian face that could only exist in a nightmare filled his vision. A foul-smelling mouth filled with wicked teeth covered his face when he tried to scream. Clawed hands ripped at his jaws and forced them open. Something cold and slimy filled his mouth and began to claw its way down his throat.

In less than a heartbeat he was underwater, feeling the thing clawing its way into his body, ripping and tearing its way past his lungs. The pain felt like a hot coal burning its way through him. Then the mouth covering his was gone and he instinctively gasped for air. Cold, clear water rushed passed his torn trachea to fill his lungs. When Sean finally lost consciousness, the creature released its grasp and let the current carry his lifeless body downstream. Its task had been completed.

Chapter 1

November, 2013

It all started when Ryan Lowell opened his email and found the invitation to his 50th high school class reunion. His heart quickened and a cold prickle of sweat erupted on his face and chest before he even opened the email and started reading.

Poquonock High School Class of 1964

Dear Classmates,

Can you believe it? Next June it will be 50 years since our graduation from Poquonock High School. We plan to mark the event with a reunion weekend. We hope you can attend all, or at least some, of the events we are planning. Things are still in flux, but plan to be with us the second weekend in October of next year if you can make it.

The Reunion Committee

Ryan reached out, was about to delete it, then thought, *What the heck? I haven't been back there since I graduated. Maybe I'll go.* It only took a few keystrokes to create a new folder, *Reunion*, and park it there.

Over the next few days, memories from high school tugged at him like a puppy on a leash. During his freshman year, someone—actually a lot of someones—had started stealing silverware from the cafeteria. Threats of detention, and finally expulsion, for the guilty parties did nothing to stop the thefts. It finally got so bad the school had to order more just so the students had enough knives and forks to eat with at lunch. Then, once the silverware bins were full of nice, new, shiny utensils, the old ones started showing back up. By the end of the year, there wasn't room for all the knives, forks, and spoons the cafeteria now had on hand. Ryan had his suspicions of who had been responsible, but the names never leaked out, and no one except the pranksters knew for sure who had pulled it off.

And how about the time he and Bobby Palcow had yanked Mr. Rich's chain with the *Animal Farm* book covers? Mr. Rich insisted that every student show him the book they intended to write their report from. He also insisted every student had to have their own copy—sharing was not allowed. When the day came for presenting the books for inspection, each student was called up to Mr. Rich's desk where he/she was required to place the book in front of him and wait for his approval, or disapproval, of their choice. Ryan had known *Animal Farm* was one of Rich's favorites, so it was an easy choice. When he saw that Bobby Palcow had also selected that particular book, inspiration had struck. Sitting next to each other at lunch, he and Bobby had drawn the same doodles on their book covers. The pig on the right got an apple in its mouth, the mule on the left got glasses and a derby hat, and finally, a spider web, complete with furry black spider, adorned the lower sec-tion along with George Orwell's name.

Since Lowell starts with an L, and Palcow starts with a P, Ryan was called to Mr. Rich's desk first. When he got there, he handed his copy of *Animal Farm* over for approval. Mr. Rich frowned at the artwork that adorned the cover, but con-gratulated him on his selection and returned it to him.

When Bobby Palcow's name was called, Bobby made a detour past Ryan's desk on his way to the front of the room. He slowed as he passed Ryan, and Ryan pretended to pass something to him.

When Bobby handed his copy of *Animal Farm* to Mr. Rich, the teacher placed the book flat on his desk, frowned up at Bobby and shook his head. "*Animal Farm*, excellent choice Mis-ter Palcow—isn't it, Mister Lowell?"

"Ah, yes, Sir," Ryan answered from his seat.

"Mister Lowell, would you bring your copy back up for a minute, please?" Mr. Rich asked, staring holes into Ryan's eyes.

"Yes, Sir," Ryan answered, and made a show of trying to find the book in his desk.

"Is there a problem, Mister Lowell," Mr. Rich asked, a hint of satisfaction in his voice.

"No, sir, I've got it," Ryan answered, and pulled his copy out of the pile of books stuffed in his desk.

"Here it is, Sir," he said, and placed it on Mr. Rich's desk alongside Bobby Palcow's. There was complete silence in the room as Mr. Rich examined both books. Both were new, never read, and both were decorated exactly the same.

"I hope you boys enjoy the books as much as you seem to have enjoyed the covers. I'll expect your reports to show as much imagination as your artwork."

When these little blasts from the past kept coming, he

knew he had to find his old yearbook.

* * *

What was I thinking, keeping all these things? I'll never read them again, and all they do is take up space, he thought as he dug through boxes of books that had sat unopened in the basement for years. *Hardcovers, paperbacks, fiction, college textbooks, everything but what I'm looking for. Where the hell is it?* As he worked, he piled the books in two stacks, one to keep and one to give away or take to the dump.

"There you are, you little devil," he said out loud when he finally located his old yearbook, the *Panther's Pride*, in the bottom of the last possible box it could be in. Somehow, it looked smaller than he remembered. Then he opened the book and he was lost in the past.

The first few pages were taken up by the Board of Education and the Administration. He only vaguely remembered them.

Next in line was the faculty, and he was surprised at how many of them he did remember. Some fondly—some not so much.

Miss Shea, in her first year of teaching English, not much older than the seniors. Short, pert, and beautiful. How many adolescent dreams had gone up in smoke when she came back to school after Christmas break with an engagement ring on her finger?

Mr. Bounan, the math teacher, who insisted they "show their work." It wasn't until years later that Ryan realized why. The guy gave partial credit for the method, so if you transposed a couple of numbers and came out with some off-the-wall answer, you could still salvage a passing grade.

And then there were his classmates, all fresh-faced and

ready to conquer the world. Yeah, right.

Ryan, Best wishes to a great guy. Be good, have fun, and keep in touch, Nancy.

Ryan, Hope you'll forget our little disagreement. I know I will. Have fun in college and leave the girls alone, Love, Linda. What disagreement? He didn't remember any disagreement. If she hadn't been smiling out at him, he might not have remembered her.

Ryan, Don't forget our sociology class. You were never awake. Best of Luck, Bruce. Was that true? Did he really sleep in class?

Here was one he did remember … Betty Hainley. She had been his first major crush in their Junior year. He wondered if she was coming to the reunion and if she would even remember him. How cruel would it be if she didn't?

And it went on. There were one hundred and forty-five kids in his graduating class, and most of them had signed his yearbook. And even though the pages peeled back the years, there were faces in there he just didn't remember. There were also faces he would never forget, guys he had hung out with, girls who still owned a piece of his heart. But there was one face, a face that had haunted him for years, that should have been there, but wasn't.

Bran.

He wasn't in the yearbook because he never made it to high school, never made it past sixth grade. And only Ryan knew why.

Ryan had tried for years to erase that face, and the memories that went with it, from his mind. But every fifteen years or so, Bran would suddenly be there for a few months—always in the summer. Sometimes he was no more than a diaphanous figure floating at the edge of Ryan's vision. Other times Ryan felt like he could reach out and touch him. But Bran was never really there. It was just Ryan's mind playing tricks.

Yes, it was time to go back to Poquonock. Time to close that chapter of his life and put some old fears, and his friend, to rest.

Chapter 2

Summer, 1956

Roger Green was not happy. His dad's car was broken and they couldn't even drive to St. Albans to go to synagogue, where he could see his old pals. *Why did my dad have to get transferred here? I've got no friends here, and it doesn't look like I'm going to find any. Nobody here wants to be friends with a Jew,* he thought as he walked down the dirt road that lead to the river. *But at least I've got these woods.*

Being a city boy, the woods were a new and wonderful experience for him. He loved the solitude and the birds that filled the trees with song or screamed at him from above. Once he even saw a deer standing in the road. He had stood quietly, hardly daring to breathe, and it seemed that they had shared a bond, if only for a minute. His favorite part was the river. It was constantly changing while it stayed the same. Things would drift by on the current; frogs filled its bank and water bugs skimmed across its surface while fish flashed just below it. Today he was sitting on the huge rock that stood in the river's path like a granite road block. Locals just called it "The Rock."

He sat at the top of the granite monolith, thirty feet above the water, tossing stones in the river. He was watching the concentric circles they made radiate out from where they hit before being deformed by the current, when something below the surface caught his eye. *What is that?* If it was a fish, it was a real monster. It had to be at least ten feet long. When it stopped swimming and settled just below the surface at The Rock's edge, he crept closer to get a better look.

What is that? he thought again as he peered over the edge of The Rock. It was just deep enough that he couldn't make out what it was. He didn't want to spook it, so he lay down to get a better look at it. When he dipped his head close to the water, the thing surged up at him. He started to jump back, but in the instant it took him to react, clawed hands grabbed him and dragged him over the edge and into the river.

As Roger struggled to free himself from the claws digging into his back, a reptilian face pressed itself into his. When his need for air forced him to open his mouth, something forced itself past his lips and down his throat. The last few minutes of Roger's life were filled with pain and fear. Then the darkness claimed him and he felt nothing.

* * *

While Roger Green was fighting for his life, Ryan Lowell and Brando Liotti were blithely unaware of the nightmare events the summer would bring.

"You got your knife with you?" Bran asked.

"Yeah," Ryan answered. Then he slipped the new pen knife he had gotten for his birthday from his pocket. It was a beauty. It had two blades, one long, one short, and a plastic handle carved to look like deer antler. Bran hadn't seen it yet. Ryan had been waiting for just the right time to bring it out and show it off.

Bran didn't rise to the bait. Instead, he said, "Good. Let's play some mumblety-peg—unless you're chicken," his friend added before Ryan could decline.

"Fine, but knuckles, not closeies," Ryan told him, knowing that Bran would have picked closeies, where the winner is the one who throws his knife and sticks it closest to his opponent's foot. Ryan was actually better than Bran at throwing his knife, but it made him nervous to toss it at his friend's foot—and Bran knew it.

Bran dug his lucky Indian Head nickel out of the small watch-pocket of his jeans. It was so worn you couldn't even see the date. "Flip ya for who goes first. You call it."

"Okay, but no dog poop," Ryan said before Bran could flip the coin.

Bran grinned, remembering the last time when he had stuck the peg in a pile of dog poop because the winner of the game got to stick a peg in the location of his choice. The loser had to pull it out with his teeth. Both boys had been getting quite creative as to where they stuck the peg, but the dog poop had been a bit over the top, at least in Ryan's opinion, since he was the one who had to pull it.

"Tails," Ryan called when Bran flicked the coin into the air. "And let it hit the ground. You always win when you catch it."

The nickel hit the ground, bounced once, spun around a few times, and flopped down, Indian head side up.

"Crap," Ryan said

"Hah, beat ya," Bran crowed, and knelt down to start the game. Then he did something that shocked his friend. He reached around his back and pulled out a hunting knife with a six-inch blade in a leather sheath.

"Hey, where did you get that?" Ryan demanded.

"Found it in the attic. I think it was my dad's," Bran answered.

Any jealousy Ryan might have felt about the knife evaporated when he found out it had been his friend's dad's. Bran's dad had died in Korea.

"Take it out," Ryan told his friend.

Bran did, and exposed the bright, shiny blade.

"Wow!" was all Ryan could say, then blurted out, "You're not using that in mumblety-peg!"

"Why not?" Bran answered, enjoying his friend's envy and fear.

"Because it's not fair," Ryan argued.

"Don't worry. I wouldn't stick this baby in the ground. I might hit a rock and ruin the blade," Bran told him as he slipped it back into its sheath. Then, taking his time because he knew Ryan was impressed, he took off his belt, threaded it through the slits on the sheath, and strapped it to his hip.

"Now, let's play," he said, knowing Ryan couldn't take his eyes off the hunting knife.

The first, and easiest, toss was "knuckles." Ryan made a fist with his right hand, thumb on top, fingers facing up, and laid the knife across them. Then he rapidly swung his hand to the right and up and over in a semicircle. The motion imparted sufficient momentum to allow the blade to stick in the ground at the end of its downward path. Bran completed it without any problems. He then repeated the same toss with his left hand. This time, the knife stuck, but barely. He could just get the two fingers under the tip of the handle that the boys required for it to be considered a good stick.

"Fingers," Ryan said, knowing Bran would have trouble with the left hand on this one.

Bran made a fist with his right hand, extended the first and pinky fingers, laid the knife across them, and repeated the throwing motion used in knuckles. When he was done, the knife was sticking almost straight up out of the ground.

"Hah!" he cried, and pulled it out for his next toss. This one didn't go so smoothly. He got the blade to enter the ground point first, but then it wobbled and flopped onto its side.

"Nice try, now watch the expert," Ryan told him. He got all the way through "chinzies," where the point of the knife is placed on the chin and held in place by one finger. The thrower then flips the knife off his chin and tries to stick it in the ground, before he missed.

Bran knew he was beat, but tried anyway. He got all the way to "headsies" before Ryan won out by "plowing the field." Plowing the field meant he had to stick his knife in the ground at a forty-five-degree angle and then slap it to make it skip across the ground. It had to stick to win.

"Now where to put this stick," Ryan teased as Bran folded his knife and slipped it into his pocket. "I know, here," he told Bran as he pointed to a mud puddle left over from last night's thunderstorm. He used a rock to pound the stick into the earth beneath the puddle. When he was done, the top of the stick was almost even with the puddle's muddy surface. The ground was soft, so it would be easy to pull out, but that wasn't the point. Bran had to pull the stick out with his teeth, and he was going to have to put his face in the muddy water to do it. "Pull it, sucker," Ryan said once it was in.

Bran flipped him the bird—something they had just learned about—and kneeled down next to the puddle. He tried to lean over to reach the stick, but it was just far enough out that he couldn't do it without falling in … face first.

"Come on, loser, pull it out," Ryan teased.

There was nothing Bran could do but stick his hands in the puddle to brace himself. Then he held his breath, lowered his face to the water, grasped the end of the stick with his teeth, and yanked it out. When he sat up, dirty water was dripping from his face, and his hands were covered in mud.

Ryan was rolling on the ground, laughing. "Got you that time," he crowed when he managed to catch his breath.

Bran threw the stick away and knelt to wash the mud off his hands. "Yeah, well next time it's closeies," he said as he wiped his hands on his jeans.

"Now what?" Ryan asked. Since he had won at mumblety-peg, it was understood that Bran got to choose what they did next.

"The Rock," Bran told him as he hopped on his bike and started pedaling hard.

"I'm not going swimming!" Ryan yelled at his friend's back. As hot as the day was, eighty-five degrees and climbing, the water was going to be cold, really cold. It came from the mountains and hadn't even started to warm up yet.

Ryan knew he could never catch Bran. He had too big a head start, and he was reckless on a bike, but Ryan peddled as hard as he could anyway. The ride was smooth and fast until he hit the last section of the old road that led to The Rock. It hadn't been used or graded in years, and it was filled with ruts and washouts. Bran flew over them like they weren't there, but Ryan slowed and picked his way to avoid the worst sections.

The Rock stood in the river's path, forcing it to make a sharp left turn. It had been worn smooth by rain, weather, and time. When Ryan reached it, Bran's bike was already lying on the ground, its back wheel still spinning. A thin cloud of dust filled the air from his friend's skidding stop. Ryan braked, got off his bike, and carefully placed it on its kickstand. Then he went to join Bran, who was probably already stripped down to his shorts and grinning like an idiot.

The Rock stuck out of the surrounding woods like the skull of some giant from ages past. Its crown rose ten feet above the old road and blocked the view of the river below. On the side that faced the river, the weather-worn granite plunged down into the river below at a thirty-degree angle that made climbing down it tricky at the best of times. When it was wet from the rain, it could be a real challenge not to take a fall and slide all the way into the river.

Ryan climbed the short path up and found Bran sitting at the top, peering down at the water, thirty feet below.

"Look! What is that?" Bran asked, pointing to something on the other side. It was almost impossible to see, hovering just below the surface in the shadows of the trees that overhung the water. Only some unnatural movement had drawn Bran's attention.

"Where? I don't see anything." Ryan answered.

Bran stood behind Ryan and pointed at the spot where he had seen something. "On the other side, right there, at the bend."

Ryan looked, and after a minute or two, he thought he might see ... something.

"See it?" Brand asked impatiently.

"Maybe, but I think it's just weeds or something," Ryan told him.

"No way," Bran answered, and scrambled back over the top of The Rock to the road where their bikes were parked. The two of them had long since picked the dirt clean of stones there, so Bran had to run back up the old road to find what he was looking for: a stone the size of an egg. He finally found one, half-buried in the hard-packed roadbed. He had to kick it out of the dirt with the heel of his sneaker, but after a few good whacks, it came free.

"Watch," he said, and then threw the stone at the spot in the river he had been pointing at. Bran had a pretty good arm, honed by throwing rocks at bottles and cans at the dump, and he managed to hit fairly close to the spot he was aiming at. There was a large splash, and then movement under the water as a large, sinuous form moved away from the bank and into the current.

"What is that?" Ryan asked,

"I don't know," Bran responded, and they both stared in wonder as the form drifted toward their side of the river.

"It's way too big to be a fish," Ryan said.

"Yeah, but what is it? Let's check it out," Bran said.

They started to scramble down The Rock's smooth, worn surface until Ryan glanced up and got a better look at the thing under the water. "Bran, wait," he cried, and grabbed his friend's arm. "Look!"

Whatever it was, it was gliding just above the bottom, becoming less distinct as the water deepened near the face of The Rock. It blended in perfectly with the bottom and they almost lost sight of it as it moved *across* the current, not with it. It shimmered and wavered, distorted by the movement of the river until it reached the face of rock where the water was deepest. Then it rose to the surface, clinging to the stone's surface with oversized claw-like hands; it lifted its head above the water and hissed at them.

Ryan broke and ran first, but Bran was hot on his heels. Then both boys were on their bikes and peddling like mad, following the old road past The Logs and The Back Beach. They didn't stop until they were at the old brick foundation they used for a fort. This time even Ryan dropped his bike as he rushed to reach its familiar interior.

The foundation was a remnant of someone's failed dream

that the boys had taken full advantage of. Unlike the poured concrete of the foundations of the development houses, it was made of brick and mortar. The brick was weathered and chipped, faded to a dull rust color by the years. It was located in the woods between Ryan's house and the dirt road that ran to The Back Beach. There were several roofless "rooms" with shattered walls. One had four intact walls and a doorway on one end. When the boys had found it, they had immediately claimed it for their own. They had spent days clearing it of the detritus that had built up in it over the years. The ceiling was open to the sky, but they had covered it with wood salvaged from a pile of debris someone had illegally dumped in the old gravel pit. When it was done, it was the perfect clubhouse. But neither of them thought "clubhouse" was the right word to describe it. After all, it was just the two of them, and they weren't a club, so they wound up calling it their fort.

Bran took his seat on the old kitchen chair he had hauled back from the dump, while Ryan sat on the brick shelf that ran along the back wall. There were several candles scattered around the floor and walls, mounted in puddles of wax that showed where others had once sat.

"Shut the door," Bran ordered, and Ryan hopped off his perch and swung the makeshift plywood door they had added closed. With it in place, the fort's interior was only lit by what little sunlight managed to peek in through cracks in the roof and around the entrance. Even on a day like today, when the temperature hit eighty-five, it was cool and a little damp inside.

"Light the candles," Ryan said, and Bran dug the pack of matches he had stolen from home out of his pocket. Ryan heard a match strike, and the sharp smell of sulfur immediately mixed with the odor of the damp earth that covered the fort's floor. In less than a minute, the interior was filled with a warm, yellow glow. It was still cool and damp, but at least they had light.

"What was that ... thing?" Ryan blurted out.

"I don't know. What did it look like to you?"

"Scary, horrible," Ryan said.

"I know that, but what did it look like?"

Ryan thought for a minute, and then said, "It was ... I don't know ... on top, it was dark, like a shark. But underneath, it was all white, like a frog's belly. That's all I remember."

"Yeah, it was like a big snake, but it had arms and hands ... but it was way too big to be a snake. Did you see those claws? And its eyes, did you see them? They were all blue. And it had really sharp teeth. I thought it *was a* snake until it opened its mouth and hissed at us. Then I saw all those teeth —but snakes don't have teeth."

"I didn't see that. I took off as soon as it came up from the bottom. Where do you think it came from?" Ryan asked.

"The lake. I bet it came up from the lake. It's deep, like that place in Scotland with the monster."

The lake was deep, Ryan had to admit that. "It looked like something from a comic book."

The boys sat in silence for what seemed like ages before Bran said, "Maybe Old Man Turcott knows what it is, he's been around forever. We could ask him."

Ryan looked at him in dismay. "Oh man, do we have to? He's creepy ..." The wail of a siren cut off what he was going to say next.

Bran was out of the fort in a flash, leaving Ryan to put out the candles and close the door. By the time Ryan reached his bike, Bran was already twenty yards away, chasing the dust cloud the police car had left in its wake.

Both boys were out of breath when they finally caught

up to it. It was parked at The Logs, with the red bubble light on top still flashing. There was already a small crowd there before them, probably from the ball field since it was too early in the season for swimming.

"What happened?" Bran asked one of the older boys at the back.

"Somebody drowned."

"Who?" he demanded.

"Don't know, but I think it was that new kid, the one from the city," the older boy responded.

Bran paced around the people gathered near the bank, trying to get a look at what was going on, but all he could see were the backs of the older kids. "Can you see anything?" he asked Ryan.

"No," Ryan answered.

"Then, let's go," Bran said as he started peddling away from the knot of people blocking their view.

Before Ryan could ask where they were going, he was looking at Bran's back. "Oh, man," he mumbled to himself, then took off after him. Within minutes they were back at The Rock.

"What are you doing?" Ryan demanded as he skidded to a stop.

"Trying to get a better look," Bran answered as he started for the path that ran along the bank of the river. All thoughts of the thing they had seen were driven out by the need to see what was happening at The Logs, a shallow spot where huge, half-buried logs spanned the expanse of the river. It was one of two places the boys could cross to the opposite bank without getting more than their sneakers wet. They arrived there just in time to watch the police pull the body from the water. It was wearing a white T-shirt, khaki pants, and sneakers. The kid's hair was cut so short that it made him look almost bald. His T-shirt was torn to ribbons and thin red streaks ran across his back from his shoulders to his waist.

* * *

Marty Erickson was the new guy on the force. He had always wanted to be a cop, but had imagined himself working in the city, not a small town in Northern Vermont with a mind-boggling population of just over five thousand souls. But it was a place to start. Maybe, after a few years, he could talk Sally into moving to New Jersey, and he could hook up with a real police department. He wanted someplace bigger, something where the only woods were in a park. Paterson or Newark, hell, even Jersey City would be better than Poquonock —or "Podunk" as he liked to call it. The only reason Marty had wound up here was that he had met and married a girl from St. Albans when he was in college. She and her family had insisted they live "close by," and this was the only cop job he could find up here.

Marty didn't fit in here in Vermont, and he knew it. What was worse, the other guys on the force knew it, too. They were all "local" boys, born and raised within twenty miles of Poquonock. He had been the butt of more than one joke, from cow tipping to snipe hunts, since he had been here. They delighted in trying to scare him with tales of Bigfoot and Champ, the Loch Ness monster of Lake Champlain. Chief Miller had even told him about a mysterious and secret creature that had invaded the river and terrorized the town back in 1939. Marty was supposed to keep it secret and take any drowned bodies to Tom Blakely's Funeral Home if the thing came back. How dumb did they think he was? But now here he was, staring at a body in the water, not wanting to get any closer to it than he had to.

Erickson was spooked. This is just what Chief Miller had said might happen someday, and now he was afraid of what he might find. *Go ahead, the kid just drowned. He fell in and either didn't know how to swim or the water was so cold he couldn't recover from the shock. He drowned. Simple as that*, he told himself. He knew he should check it out, but he just stood where he was, swaying slightly from side to side as if responding to a breeze only he could feel.

"You gonna do something ... or what?" a stick-thin man holding a fishing pole asked him.

"Yeah," someone else chimed in from the small crowd that had gathered.

In truth, he didn't want to scramble down that bank and out onto those logs. He had spent an hour shining his shoes last night and the thought of getting them all scuffed up or covered in mud disgusted him. "Okay, okay, step back," he finally said, and started down the shallow bank toward the river. He slipped and almost fell on his ass; a shower of loose pebbles tumbled down the slope and splashed into the water.

"Fuck," he mumbled to himself as he tried to walk across the logs toward the body. Their bark was long gone, and the bare wood was slippery as hell where the river flowed over them. The kids who crossed here usually did it barefoot with their pants rolled up, but he didn't think of that in time to save himself from slipping off and getting his legs wet halfway to his knees. If the dead kid hadn't been there, he was sure he would have heard laughter from the bank.

He thought about trying to climb back onto the log, but could just see himself slipping off again and going ass-over-teakettle into the river. That would give the crowd on the bank something to talk about. Instead, he gave up and concentrated on making his way to the body. He'd deal with his shoes later.

The body was lying face down in the water, pinned against a log by the slight current. As he approached it, he could see the boy's T-shirt was in tatters. There were deep, thin cuts across his back. When he reached the body, he took a deep breath and steeled himself for he what he might see when he saw its face. *Please let this be just a simple drowning,* he thought as he started to roll the body over. When he saw the terrified look frozen on the kid's face, he dropped the body and stepped back. This was not a simple drowning. This was *exactly* what the Chief had warned him about. He had thought it was a bad joke, something to scare the city boy, but it wasn't. He also remembered what else Miller had said: "If it ever happens, *do not* let the body go anywhere but Tom Blakely's Funeral Home. He'll know what to do with it."

As he stood over the body, he looked back at the bank to see if anyone else might have seen what he saw. That's when he noticed the two boys peering at him through the brush at the side of the path leading back toward The Rock.

* * *

Erickson left the body where it was until the ambulance arrived. Then he moved the onlookers far enough back that no one would be able to get a good look at the body. Since he was already wet to his knees, he dragged it to the bank by himself. "Help me get him out of the water," he told the driver and his partner when he got it there.

The men were quick and efficient. They placed the body in a basket stretcher and covered it with a sheet before loading it into the back of the ambulance. Erickson thought the three of them were the only ones who saw the deep gashes and the look on the dead boy's face before they had him loaded into the ambulance.

"Did you see his face?" Tim Sloat, the younger man said. "It looks like something scared the daylights out of him."

"I guess you'd be pretty scared, too, if you thought you were drowning," Erickson told him.

"Yeah, well this isn't the first floater I've seen, and none of them looked like that. And what about those cuts? How did he get those?"

"Tree branches, rocks on the river bottom, who knows?" Erickson said, grasping for any excuse he could think of. "The coroner will figure that out. That's his job, not ours."

Sloat started to reply, but Paul Spirko, the driver, cut him off. "Come on, Tim, time's a-wasting; let's get him over to the morgue in St. Albans."

"No," Erickson blurted out. "Take him to Blakely's Funeral Parlor and don't tell anyone about the condition of the body."

Spirko frowned and shook his head, "We can't do that. We have to take him to the morgue. The medical examiner is going to have to see him."

Erickson was scrambling. If he let these guys take the kid to St. Albans, the chief would have his ass. It might even cost him his job. "The medical examiner can see him at Blakely's," Erickson told him. "This kid is not leaving town. After the medical examiner sees him, Tom Blakely can fix his face so his parents don't have to see him like this. If he goes to the morgue, this will be all over the news. I don't want to do that to his people."

Spirko didn't like it, but he agreed. "Fine, if you say so. But it's your ass if we get in trouble for this."

"No problem," Erickson answered.

Spirko nodded and handed Erickson a clipboard and a pen. "Damn right, no problem, and just to make sure it's no problem, I need you to put it in writing." Erickson took the clipboard to do just that, but had to wait until his hands stopped shaking before he could write it down. Then he handed the clipboard back to Spirko and told them he would follow them to the Funeral Home. When they pulled into Blakely's parking lot, he was right behind them.

"Wait here while I go in and talk to Tom," he told them. Then he went to make sure Blakely knew what to do and say to the men when they brought the body in. He didn't have to do much explaining. As soon as he told Blakely a kid had drowned in the river and they had the body outside, the man started giving him directions.

"Bring him around back and I'll meet you there," Blakely said, and then he was gone.

What the hell? Erickson thought, and went back out to tell the driver what to do.

"Drive around the back, Blakely will meet you there," he told Spirko through his open window.

"You got it," Spirko replied.

In less than a minute the ambulance and the cruiser were parked behind the funeral home, out of sight from Main Street. Tom Blakely was waiting for them in front of a set of double doors.

"Bring him right in here," he told Sloat and Spirko. "I'll take it from there."

"Sure thing," Spirko replied, and they wheeled the stretcher carrying the body into the back of the funeral home.

"Put him right there," Blakely directed them, pointing to a stainless steel table.

"You're going to need to sign for the body," Spirko said, handing him a clipboard that had been balanced on the sheet covering the corpse. It was the same one he had had Marty use, and the note directing him to deliver the body to the funeral home was still clipped to it.

"Of course," Blakely responded as he took the clipboard and scribbled his name on the transfer slip.

After the body was moved, he thanked the men and told them, "Please close the doors on your way out."

Spirko was going to respond, but Blakely had already turned his attention to the body.

After they heard the doors close, Erickson looked at the mortician and asked, "What the fuck, Tom?"

"This has happened before," Blakely answered, ignoring his question. "Has anyone else seen this besides those two?"

"The people at The Logs saw the body, but not his face or the gashes."

"That's good," Blakely replied.

"Wait," Erickson said, "There were two kids on the path next to the river. They had a different angle on things, they might have seen something."

"Kids? What, teenagers?"

"No, young kids. Maybe ten or eleven. Couldn't be any older."

"Well, you better find out," Blakely told him. "If they did see something, and they start talking about it, there are folks in town who just might listen."

"So, it's just two kids. Who listens to kids?"

"The old timers who were here the last time this happened will listen. They'll ignore it if they can, but not if it slaps them in the face."

"What the hell is going on here, Tom?" Erickson demanded.

"Talk to the Chief. He knows more than I do. So just talk to him."

* * *

"Chief, the kid in the river," Erickson said as he walked

into the Chief's office.

"Yeah?" Chief Brad Miller said.

"It was ... weird," Marty responded, dreading what he had to say next.

The chief must have sensed what was coming because he told Erickson to shut the door and take a seat. After he did, Miller said, "Weird? How?"

"The kid's face—it was horrible. His mouth was open and it looked like he died screaming. And he had cuts—no, slashes—all over his back and chest, like someone had taken a straight razor to him."

Miller looked across at him with a sick look on his face. "Shit. It's back."

"What's back?" Marty demanded. When Miller didn't answer right away, he said, "You know, I always thought all that stuff you told me about was bull shit, just something to screw with the new guy, but it wasn't, was it?"

"No, I wish it was, but it isn't. Who else knows about it?"

"Tom Blakely. He has the body at his funeral home. He says he'll clean it up and fix the face before anyone else has access to it."

"That's good—for this one," the Chief said, "but what about the next one? Because there sure as hell will be a next one if we don't kill this thing first."

"I don't understand. What's the big deal about keeping this a secret?" Erickson asked.

"The same reason we kept it secret the last time. If it gets out there's some kind of 'monster' in the river, folks in town will panic. People from all over will show up with guns, and who knows what else, to go hunting for the thing. It'll be a fucking circus and somebody, maybe a lot of somebodies, is bound to get shot. We're going to handle this in-house."

"How did they get rid of it the last time?" Erickson asked.

"Ask Dave Longo. He was there, but he's never talked about it as far as I know."

"Our Dave Longo? Fat Dave Longo?" Erickson asked incredulously.

"Yeah, Dave Longo. He wasn't always fat. He was a hell of a cop back in the day. You could learn a lot from him. You want to know about the thing in the river, you need to talk to Dave."

Chapter 3

The boys were back in the confines of their fort, admiring Bran's hunting knife, when Bran brought up the dead kid and the thing in the water. "I'm telling you, first we see that thing at The Rock, and then there's a dead kid at The Logs. That thing killed him," Bran insisted.

"You really think so?" Ryan asked.

"Yeah, don't you?"

Ryan shook his head, "I don't know—I don't think I want to know."

"Well, I do, and I'm going to find out," Bran told him.

"Yeah, how?"

"We gotta talk to Old Man Turcott."

"No way, man, he gives me the creeps. You want to talk to him, you talk to him. I'm not going near that guy."

"What's wrong with him? Why's he give you the creeps?" Bran demanded. The old man gave him the creeps, too, but he wasn't about to let Ryan know that.

"Man, he just looks creepy. He walks around town and looks like he's mad all the time. I've never even seen him smile. He always needs a shave … and I'll bet he smells bad, too."

* * *

Bran pestered Ryan about going to see Old Man Turcott until his friend finally gave in. It was a routine they were both used to. Ryan was naturally more cautious than Bran, but Bran could talk him into just about anything if he kept at him.

When Ryan finally gave in, he still had one condition. "Fine, I'll go with you, but I'm not talking to him. You'll have to do that."

"Why, you chicken?" Bran said.

"No," Ryan countered. "I just don't want to."

"Then let's shoot for it. Loser has to knock on his door and ask him. Unless you're chicken."

"I'm not chicken," Ryan snapped, then got ready to play Bran's game. He wasn't worried because he beat Bran three out of four times whenever they played odds and evens.

"Once, twice, three—shoot," Bran counted. On "shoot," Ryan called out "evens" and thrust out two fingers. At the same time Bran called "odds" and thrust out one. Ryan felt sick to his stomach when he saw that he had lost.

"Odds," Bran laughed, "you lose."

* * *

The boys stood in front of Old Man Turcott's house while Ryan tried to build up the courage to actually go up and knock on the door. Neither he nor Bran had gotten off their bike yet, so they were still poised to make a quick getaway if they had to.

31

"You lost—knock," Bran demanded, and he gave Ryan a shove.

"All right, all right," Ryan practically whined as he got off his bike and set the kickstand. Bran had to give him another shove to get him moving toward the house. His desire to be somewhere else, anywhere else, grew with each step he took toward Old Man Turcott's house. He actually thought he might faint as he climbed the steps to the screened-in porch.

His heart was hammering as he raised his hand to knock on the battered screen door. He paused for a second and let it drop, wondering why he let Bran trick him into this. "I can't," he admitted.

"Chicken," Bran said, and then he ran over, bounded up the steps, and rapped three times on the door. Ryan stood there, dumbfounded as Bran jumped off the porch and ran back to the safety of his bike. He was on it and ready to take off before the door stopped rattling.

Ryan was getting ready to run, too, when a grizzled, unshaven face appeared behind the screen. "What do you want, boy?" Old Man Turcott demanded before Ryan could get his feet to move.

"Well?" the man demanded when Ryan didn't answer.

Ryan fidgeted before answering "We saw some ..." Ryan said before the old man cut him off.

"Spit it out, boy, I ain't got all day for foolishness."

"We ..." Ryan started to say again before Bran came halfway to the house and broke in. "We saw something weird in the river and want to know if you know what it is," he said from the safety of the lawn.

The old man considered the boys for a moment before answering. "What kind of weird thing?"

"Something that wasn't human," Bran told him.

"That right, boy?" Turcott asked Ryan, staring straight into the boy's eyes.

"Yes, sir," Ryan answered.

"When did you see this thing?" the old man asked.

"Yesterday. We saw it at The Rock. And there was a dead kid at The Logs. We think that thing killed him," Bran said.

The old man didn't say anything for a full minute, and then he shook his head and said, "Well, then you boys better stay away from that river."

"Do you know what it was?" Bran asked, coming closer to the porch.

"Nope," the man answered, looking him straight in the eyes.

When it became apparent the man wasn't going to tell them anything else, Bran said, "Come on, Ryan, let's go," and waited for his friend before turning to leave.

When they turned to leave, Old Man Turcott spoke again before closing the door. "You boys stay away from that river or you could wind up killed, too."

Ryan was the first to break and run for his bike, but Bran was right behind him.

* * *

Turcott's hands were shaking as he watched the boys ride away on their bikes. Of course he knew what the thing they had seen in the river was. He had killed it once, back in '39, just like his father had killed it in 1899. But the damn thing kept coming back. It always came back.

He thought the one named Ryan would probably stay away from the river, but the other one, Bran, he wouldn't. That boy had fire in his eyes and a chip on his shoulder. That one was going to get himself killed if someone didn't kill the creature first. Well, it wasn't going to be him this time. Maybe it would be Longo.

His hands were still shaking when he poured two inches of rye whiskey into the jelly jar he used as a glass. They didn't break as easy as a real glass when you dropped them.

Two drinks later he got up, walked to the bathroom, took off his shirt, and looked into the mirror. It was the first time in ten years he had looked at himself with his shirt off. Thin, pale scars crisscrossed his chest. He couldn't see the ones that ran across his back, but he knew they were there. He cringed at the sight of them and cursed himself for being a coward. Then he went back and poured himself another drink.

Chapter 4

Marty Erickson watched Dave Longo walk to the middle of the street and hold up his arms to stop traffic. Then, when he deemed it safe, he told the kids standing on the sidewalk that they could cross. They crossed in little groups by age, the bigger kids in front, the middle graders next, and the little kids last. Once they were all safely across, Longo allowed the cars to go on their way. When they were gone, he walked back to the sidewalk and waited for the next group of kids to gather. Erickson couldn't believe the fat cop in the wrinkled uniform had ever been more than a crossing guard.

He was damned if he was going to ask him about whatever it was that had killed that kid in the river. He would, however, ask him if he knew who the kids were that he had seen on the bank.

What Erickson didn't know was that Longo wasn't all that impressed with him either. Longo thought the man was a bit too high on himself. His uniform was always perfectly pressed, his shoes spit-shined, and he walked like he had a stick up his ass. He was a city boy who was never going to fit in with the locals. And here he was, strutting up to him like he owned the world.

"Dave, I'm looking for a couple of kids. Maybe you can tell me who they are."

"What makes you think I'll know who they are?" Longo asked.

"Come on, Dave, you've got to know who these kids are. You've been the crossing guard at Poquonock Elementary since God made little green apples."

Asshole, Dave thought before answering. "Marty, a lot of kids go to Poquonock Elementary. What are you looking for these two for?"

"I saw them at The Logs when I was dragging that kid's body from the river. You know, the one that drowned. They were on the path that goes up to that big rock. The dead kid had to have floated down from there. I want to ask those two if they saw or heard anything. Maybe they saw him fall in. Maybe they heard him call for help. I'm just trying to figure out what happened."

Dave thought for a minute before responding. He wanted to be sure he had the right kids in mind before he said anything. To the kids, he was just the fat cop who stopped traffic for them at the school crossing. Old-timers in town knew he was a lot more than that. Back in the day, he had been one hell of a cop. The summer of '39 changed all that.

"Marty, you really think they saw something?" Dave asked.

"I don't know. They took off before I could talk to them."

"Can you tell me what they look like?"

"Small, thin, and they both had brown hair. One of them has a buzz cut, the other one has a flattop. They were both wearing polo shirts and dungarees."

Dave thought for another minute before answering. "It sounds like Ryan Lowell and Brandon Liotti. They go everywhere together."

"They still here?"

"Nah, they went home a while ago."

"You know where they live?"

"No, but you can get that from the school," Dave told him.

When Marty turned to leave, Dave stopped him with a hand on his shoulder. "Was there anything weird about the kid that drowned?"

"What do you mean … weird?"

"Just … weird," Dave said.

Marty thought about the kid's face and the cuts on the body and a shiver went through his body. "No, Dave, nothing weird. He just drowned. Why?"

"No reason," Dave answered, but he knew Marty was lying. He stared at Erickson's back as the man walked away and had a very bad feeling about that drowning.

* * *

When Erickson got back to the station after talking to Longo, Tom Blakely was there talking to the Chief. Miller looked up, saw Erickson through the glass window of his office and motioned him inside.

"Close the door," the Chief said when Marty joined them.

"We've identified the kid you pulled out of the river," Miller told him. "His name was Roger Green. His family's new in town, and they're Jewish. Maybe that's why the kid was in the woods by himself. Anyway, they don't want an autopsy because of their religious beliefs, and that's their right. They'll do whatever Jews do, and the burial will follow right after that."

"And that's good?" Erickson asked.

"Yes, it is," Blakely answered. "Believe me, if there was an autopsy, we'd never keep a lid on this. The papers and the State Police would be all over it."

"So right now the only ones who know about this are the three of us and Dave Longo," Miller told Blakely.

"Dave knows? That's good," Blakely said. "He'll know what to do about this."

Erickson stayed to talk to Miller after Blakely left. "Chief, I didn't tell Longo about this," he admitted once the undertaker was gone.

"Why not? I thought I told you to talk to him."

Erickson was not about to admit that he didn't think he needed to take any advice from a fat has-been. Instead, he said, "I thought you wanted to keep this between you, me, and Blakely."

"Well, you thought wrong. Talk to Dave, first thing tomorrow."

Chapter 5

Summer, 1939

Dave Longo was sitting in Guy's Diner enjoying a cup of coffee and a piece of apple pie when the phone behind the counter rang. The diner was one of those new stainless steel ones that could be delivered to a site and set up in days. It never would have made it in a town as small as Poquonock if the paper mill hadn't been there. Workers from the mill made up most of the breakfast and lunch crowd.

Longo was half of the Poquonock police department. The other half was Chief Don Miller. Miller was the Chief because he had been there longer. In fact, he had been the only police officer in Poquonock until the town council had authorized a second officer. It had helped that the paper mill had offered to pay the second officer's salary as a goodwill gesture to the town. The loggers and mill workers were a wild bunch and caused most of the trouble Miller and Longo had to deal with.

When they had made the offer in '35, Dave had been the

obvious choice. He had joined the army in '31 when he was twenty and had spent four years in the service, the last two in the Military Police. He was getting ready to re-enlist and make a career out of the Army when his mother wrote him about the decision to add an officer to the Poquonock police force. Home had won out over a life in the service of Uncle Sam, and here he was.

"Guy's," Dave heard Joe Guy say into the phone's mouth-piece. "Yeah, he's here. You want to talk to him?"

"It's for you," Joe told Dave, and motioned to the phone.

Dave looked longingly at the pie, put down his fork, and walked around the counter to take the call. "This is Longo."

"Dave, John Weiss says there's a body in the river. I need you to go down and check it out," the Chief told him.

"Where is it?" Longo asked.

"Right by that big rock where the kids swim. You know, the one near the dirt road that runs back there. John's at the call box on the corner of Main and Colfax. Pick him up there and he'll take you to the body."

"Right, Chief, I'll get right down there," Longo told him, and handed the phone back to Joe. Then he looked longingly at the coffee and pie and said, "Sorry, Joe, I've gotta leave."

"Dave, hang on a minute," Joe said, and poured the coffee in a paper to-go cup. Then he wrapped the pie in wax paper and put it in a paper bag along with a fork. "Just bring the fork back next time," he said as he handed Longo the bag.

Dave doubted he'd have a chance to eat the pie, but he took it anyway. He drank the coffee on the way.

Weiss was sitting on the curb, leaning back against a phone pole under the blue light and the red police call box. He was in his fifties now and starting to show the wear of a life lived hard. His sandy hair was rapidly receding from a high forehead and he walked with a limp from a piece of shrapnel he had picked up in France. A fishing pole and a creel sat next to him on the pavement. When Longo pulled to a stop next to him, he remained seated and spoke into the open window. "Morning, Dave."

"Morning, John." In a town as small as theirs, everybody knew everybody else. Right now Poquonock was one main street, named Main Street, of course, and two dozen or so side streets, the longest of which, Sullivan Avenue, was only four blocks long. It had a total population of less than two thousand.

"The Chief said you found a body in the river?" It was more of a question than a statement.

"Creepiest damn thing I've ever seen," Weiss answered. "I was going to drag it out of the water, but once I saw its face, I thought to hell with that. I left it where it was."

"John, you fought in the war, right? What could be worse than that?" Longo asked.

"I don't know. I've seen worse, that's for sure, but this just gave me the willies. Maybe it's because he's just a kid — no, that's not it. It was the look on his face. That kid looked like he was scared to death. What could scare a kid to death?"

"Scared to death?"

"I don't want to talk about it," Weiss told him. "I'm just going to take you to him, and then be on my way. I don't think I'll be going back there for a while after that."

"Okay," Dave answered. "Hop in and show me where it is. The Chief said it was down by that big rock, that right?"

Weiss hesitated as if unwilling to join Dave in the car. It was obvious he didn't want to go back to The Rock, but he didn't want to look like a coward, either. "Yeah," John finally answered as he rose to his feet, wincing from the pain in his hip. He got in the car and stared out the window. They drove in silence.

* * *

"There it is," Weiss said, pointing to the body. It was caught in the branches of a fallen tree. The spring flood had undercut the bank and trees were down here and there along the length of the river.

Dave looked at the body and knew there was no way of getting it out of the river by himself. It looked like it was tangled up pretty good, and it was being held there by the current. Turning to John, he said, "How about giving me a hand getting him out?"

"Nope, that's your job. I'm not going anywhere near him," Weiss answered. "You can take it from here." Then he went back to the patrol car, retrieved his pole and creel from the back seat, and started the hike back to town.

Dave stood with his hands on his hips, staring down at the body, trying to decide if he should attempt getting it out himself, or go back to the station for some help. As he watched, something moving under the surface caught his eye. It moved against the current—that's the only reason he noticed it. Then, impossibly, it stopped and slowly rose to the surface. A serpentine face stared at Dave. He had only had a fleeting glance at it, but he had an impression of ice-blue eyes, a blunt, scaly-looking face, and a sense of malice about it. He had no idea *what* he was looking at, but the damn thing spooked him, sent shivers up his spine. He felt like a rabbit staring into the eyes of a rattlesnake. It was only there for a second, and then it retreated to the bottom and moved up-stream. Dave stood rooted to the spot until it was gone. *No way in hell I'm going into the river to drag the body out by myself. Not with that thing down there. I hate to leave the body alone, but what else can I do?*

The dirt road was narrow, but Dave backed his police car to the edge of the ditch running alongside it and just managed to get turned around so he could head back the way he had come. He hadn't driven more than a quarter mile when he caught up to Weiss.

When Weiss moved out of the way to let him pass, Dave stopped next to him and asked, "John, you want a ride back?"

Weiss didn't answer; he just shook his head and waved Dave on.

"John, did you see anything weird back there? I mean, besides the body?" Dave asked.

This time, Weiss did answer. "I don't want to talk about it. I just want to get back to town."

"Well, get in then. I can have you back there in five minutes. Or," Dave added, "you can walk back. It's up to you."

Weiss looked nervously back down the road toward The Rock before placing his pole and creel in the back seat and climbing in beside Dave.

Once again, they rode in silence. Then, just before they reached his house on Main Street, Weiss said, "I saw something nasty in the river, next to the body."

Longo didn't answer, didn't prod; instead, he waited, letting Weiss tell him at his own pace.

"You saw him. He was caught in that tree. I went down to the bank to get a better look, and I saw something, some *thing* in the water next to him. It wasn't human. It glared at me with these bright blue eyes, and then it opened its mouth. That's when I thought, *Sorry, kid, I'm out of here.* I looked back when I got to the top of The Rock, and it was still there, still underwater, and staring at me. I only went back there to show you where it was. I'm not going back there again."

* * *

When Dave got back to the station, he made his way straight to the Chief's office. The station had been expanded to two rooms in the Town Hall when he was hired. Dave's office, as he liked to call it, was a fifteen by fifteen foot box. One door led directly to the parking lot. On the opposite side of the room, a second door led to the chief's windowless office. Dave didn't have much privacy, but at least he had a window.

"We have to talk," Dave said after he entered the Chief's domain and closed the door.

Miller shot a "what the fuck" look at the closed door, and said, "Did you see Weiss? Was there really a body in the river?"

"Yes, but there was *something* else there, too," Dave told him.

Miller rocked back in his chair and stared at Dave. "What do you mean, something else?"

"Something … else. I know this is going to sound crazy, but Weiss saw it, too. I don't know what to call it, a creature maybe, but it wasn't human, and I've never seen an animal like it."

"Tell me about this *something*," Miller told him.

"Just that … something," Dave repeated. "I was standing at the top of The Rock and the thing, it was underwater when I first saw it, rose to the surface. It was only there for a second, but I swear to God it scared the hell out of me."

"What did this *thing* look like?" Miller asked with a touch of sarcasm in his voice.

"It had big, ice-blue eyes. I mean the entire eye, not just

the iris. Its face looked like—I don't know—a snake, or a snake-man. I think it had scales. I felt like the God-damned thing was peering into my soul."

"Come on, Dave, this is sounding pretty weird."

"I don't care. I saw what I saw. And Weiss saw it, too."

Miller considered the possibility that Weiss and Longo were pulling his leg, having a little fun at his expense. Maybe a little payback for the box of donuts he had set on Dave's desk back on April Fool's Day. When Dave opened the box, there was a big old fake spider in it instead of donuts. He had taken Dave out for lunch later to make up for it, but maybe this was his payback.

"So the body's still there?" he asked.

"Yes."

"Then let's go and get it," the Chief said, waiting to see what Dave had planned.

* * *

"There it is," Dave said, pointing to the body that was still caught up in the branches of the fallen tree. When Miller saw it, he had to admit that this was not some elaborate practical joke at his expense.

"And where's this *thing* you saw?" the Chief asked.

"When Weiss saw it, it was right near the body. When I saw it, it was heading upstream," Longo told him, pointing in the direction the thing had gone.

"Well, I don't see anything now, so let's get that body out of the water," the Chief told him.

"Right," Dave answered, feeling uncomfortable. Then he carefully started climbing down The Rock toward the bank, shifting his gaze back and forth between the body and the spot he had last seen the thing in the water.

When they got there, Miller looked at the tree lying half in and half out of the water and decided Longo was the one who was going to make his way out to the body. "I'll hold the rope, you go get him," he told Dave. Longo took it and made his way toward the body thinking, *Well, rank does have its privileges.*

"Loop it under his shoulders if you can," Miller called when Dave reached it.

Dave didn't answer; he was trying to watch the body and the water and still keep his balance on the tree. When he was ready, he reached down, grabbed the kid by the back of his shirt, and tried to lift him. He got the body about a foot out of the water, and then something yanked back. Dave was so startled he let go and almost lost his balance. While he was doing that, the body sank back into the river. This time, the whole thing went under.

"Damn, Dave, what happened?" Miller yelled.

"Something grabbed it from below," Dave shouted as he scrambled back off the tree. Then, just before he reached the safety of the bank, a thin, sinuous arm erupted from the river and grabbed him. Fire erupted in his calf as needle-sharp claws ripped into his leg. He pulled himself free with Miller's help, but his pants were shredded and his leg was bleeding.

"Jesus Christ," the Chief yelled, and fired his revolver into the water until the hammer clicked on an empty cylinder.

They both gaped at the spot the arm had erupted from. There was no sign of the struggle that had just taken place.

"There," the Chief pointed, and Dave looked downriver to see the body floating in the current. "It'll stop when it hits The Logs. Let's go."

Dave followed the Chief up The Rock, then to the car, leaving a trail of blood in his wake. His heart was pumping frantically and he wouldn't feel the pain until later.

They got to The Logs well before the body and watched it tumble in the current as it bumped along the shallow bottom. It got hung up a few times, but neither Dave nor the Chief was willing to venture into the river to retrieve it. When it finally lodged up against The Logs, Dave looked at the Chief and said, "You stay here and cover me, I'll get him."

"You sure?" the Chief answered. "Looks like you're cut pretty bad."

Dave looked down at his leg and shrugged. "No sense both of us getting hurt. Besides, you're a better shot than I am. And you'll be more help to me than I'd be to you if something happened." The Chief wasn't as tall as Longo, five-foot-eight to Dave's six feet, but he was stockier and probably outweighed Longo by twenty pounds. Some of it was fat, but most of it was still muscle, and he was quick for a man his size.

"True enough," Miller answered. "Go, but be quick."

"No shit," Dave muttered as he jumped into the river. The water was only ankle deep, so he got to the body in a matter of seconds. Blood trailed downstream in swirling ribbons, but Dave ignored it. He had the body back to the bank in minutes.

"Oh sweet Jesus," the Chief said when Dave dropped the body in front of him. The face was frozen in a rictus of pain or fear, and deep, long cuts covered its chest and back.

Chapter 6

Poquonock High School Class of 1964

Dear Classmates,

Plans for the reunion are shaping up nicely. The dates have been set. We'll be getting together the week-end of the 10th, 11th, and 12th, of October, 2014. For those of you who can arrive on Friday, we've arranged for a tour of the high school in the morning and atten-dance at the football game in the evening.

The school has grown since we graduated and we think you'll be amazed at the difference. We've also arranged for a special seating section at the game on Friday night. That's right — the new football field now has lights. They were added in 2001. Come cheer the Poquonock Warriors to victory. After the game, we'll be gathering at Papa's Pizza for locally brewed beer and, of course, pizza.

On Saturday, we'll have a buffet style dinner at the Villa Roma from 7:00 pm to 11:00 pm. A local

DJ has been hired and will play music from the 50s, 60s, and 70s. The cost for dinner is $70.00 per person.

Please fill out the attached registration form and send it to Jennifer Skaggs along with a check for the number of people who will be attending.

See you in October!

The Reunion Committee

Thoughts of Bran, and what had happened to him, jumped into his mind. Ryan felt his resolve falter and he hit the delete button. *Fuck that! I'm never going back there … ever.*

* * *

Over the next few days, thoughts of going back to Poquonock haunted him. There had been good times there, too. The resilience of youth had gotten him past what happened in 1956. The trauma had never really left him—it was probably the reason he was still single—but he had learned to live with it. Maybe now was the time to put it to rest for once and for all. But first, he needed to know if the creature in the river was truly dead, or if it was still there, waiting for him to return.

Chapter 7

Summer, 1956

Marty Erickson parked his police car next to Longo's 1953 Ford Custom and waited for the last kid to cross the road. He was not happy that he had to go begging for advice from Longo.

"Hey, Dave, got a minute?" he asked through his open window when Longo approached him.

"Sure, Marty. What do you need?" Longo replied.

"Climb in so we can talk."

Dave got in the car with a puzzled look on his face. He knew Erickson wasn't a big fan of his, and it wasn't like him to invite Dave to talk.

"It's about that kid that drowned in the river," Erickson told him, and watched as Longo visibly flinched in his seat.

"What about him?" Longo finally asked after an awkward silence.

"It was strange. He looked like he had been scared to death and had a bunch of gashes on his chest and back. The

50

Chief said I should talk to you about it."

Longo shook his head and slumped further down in his seat. "He did, did he?" he finally asked.

"Yeah, he did," Marty answered. "He said you knew more about this than anybody."

It took Dave a minute, but he finally started talking. "The same thing happened back in the summer of '39. John Weiss … he's long gone, moved to Florida that fall … came across a body in the river. He was trout fishing, and he was good at it, too, until that day. I don't think he ever went trout fishing again after that. Anyway, when he got closer, he saw something in the river, something that scared him, and he high-tailed it back to town and called the station from the first call box he came to. The Chief sent me to investigate."

"What do you mean … something that scared him?" Erickson interrupted.

"I'll get to that," Dave answered. "Just let me tell it the way it happened.

"Anyway, I met John at the call box and he told me where the body was. It was caught up in a fallen tree by the big rock where the kids swim. Hell, I swam there when I was a kid. I had him come with me to show me where it was. He wasn't too happy about that, but he finally agreed. When we got to where he had seen the body, the only thing John would do was point at it from the top of The Rock. Then he turned tail and started walking back to town."

"So what did you do then?" Erickson asked.

"I was going to try and get the body myself, and then I saw the thing in the water and knew why John had refused to help me retrieve the body."

"What do you mean … *thing*?"

"Thing … monster … creature … whatever you want to call it. The damn thing came to the surface and grinned at me. It scared the piss out of me, let me tell you."

"A creature?" Erickson said, having a hard time believing what he was hearing.

"Yes, a creature," Longo answered. "Later, Chuck Turcott told us it was an *oniare*—anyway, I went back to the station and told the Chief. Then the two of us went back to get the body. Miller didn't believe Weiss and I had seen what we had seen, but he found out for himself soon enough.

"When we got to The Rock, the body was still there, hung up on that tree. I looked everywhere, but the thing was gone.

"'Well, let's get him,' Miller said to me, and I knew I had to do it.

"'Just keep your eyes out for the thing Weiss and I saw,' I told him.

"'Sure', he answered, but I know he thought I was blowing smoke up his ass."

Erickson started to say something, but Longo held up his hand to stop him.

"We went down to the tree and Miller watched from the bank as I climbed out on the tree's trunk to try and reach the kid. I managed to do it without falling in, but when I grabbed the kid's shirt and tried to pull him up, something pulled back. I was so shocked I let go, and the body was dragged completely under. *Fuck this*, I thought and headed back to shore. Just before I got there, a clawed hand came out of the water and grabbed my leg. If Miller hadn't caught my hand and pulled me to shore, the damn thing might have gotten me, too."

"It grabbed you?" Erickson said, skepticism obvious in his voice.

"Yeah, it grabbed me," Longo told him, and pulled up his pant leg to show Marty the nasty-looking scars that ran from just below his knee to his ankle. There were five of them. Each one stood out like a thin streak of red against his fish-belly white skin.

"Jesus, you're not kidding," Erickson said when he saw Longo's leg.

"Not for a second," Longo assured him.

"Dave, do you think those kids might have seen it?"

Longo thought for a minute before answering. "Maybe. I guess you're going to have to ask them."

"Okay, what time do they get out this afternoon? I can ask them then if you can show me who they are."

"I usually get here at a quarter to three. The kids get out at three. Be here then and I'll see what I can do."

* * *

"There they are, those two," Longo told Erickson as Brandon and Ryan came toward the school crossing.

Erickson studied the boys as they approached. They were like bookends: both were about four feet eight inches tall, slim but not skinny, and had brown hair. When they got closer, he could see that one of them sported a rash of freckles on his cheeks and nose. The one with the freckles had a butch haircut, the other one had a flattop.

"Thanks, Dave, I'll take it from here," Marty told him.

Dave nodded, but didn't leave. He wanted to hear what the kids had to say.

"Can I talk to you for a minute, boys?" Erickson asked.

"I guess so," Freckles answered, but then Flattop stepped in front of him and said, "What for?"

"I saw you boys at The Logs last Saturday. That was you, wasn't it?" Erickson asked.

"Maybe. Why?" Flattop wanted to know.

"I need to know if you saw or heard anything … unusual,"

Erickson told him.

The boys looked at each other, but neither said anything.

"Well?" Erickson asked.

"We ..." Freckles started to say, and then Erickson interrupted him.

"Wait, which one are you, Brandon, or Ryan?" Erickson asked.

"Ryan," Freckles answered.

"Okay, then you're Brandon," he said to Flattop. "Now, tell me, what did you see?"

Ryan looked to Bran as if unsure what to say. An unspoken agreement seemed to pass between them, and then Bran answered.

"Nothing, we were in our fort when we saw the police car go by. We followed it to The Logs. We couldn't see anything so we rode up to The Rock and walked back on the path to get a better look."

"And you didn't see anything ... weird?"

The boys shared another look, and Ryan said, "No, sir."

"Okay. Well, thanks, boys," Erickson said and let them go.

"Do you believe them?" Erickson asked after the boys were gone.

Of course, they were lying. You blew it. Ryan was about to tell you what they saw until you cut him off. You should have listened to him when you had the chance.

"Sure. Why would they lie?" Dave answered.

Chapter 8

Bran sat on his front porch, opening and closing his pen-knife. Ryan was gone for the day, visiting his grandmother, and Bran was bored with a capital B. There were some other kids he could play with, but it wouldn't be the same. He and Ryan were a pair—Tonto and the Lone Ranger—Batman and Robin. He didn't want to hang around with anybody else.

He flicked the blade open and looked at his bike. Without Ryan to hang with, his thoughts returned to the thing they had seen in the river.

Then he fingered the hunting knife on his belt and thought, *I'm going to find that thing, and when Ryan gets back he's going to be amazed.* As soon as the thought was in his head, he was off the porch and running for his bike. He was going to head for the river. His first stop would be The Rock.

Bran coasted to a stop in the same place he had dropped his bike when he and Ryan had been there the previous week. This time, he crept to the top of The Rock like an Indian in a John Wayne movie. When he reached the top, he scanned the river below for any sign of the *creature*, as he had started to call it. After five minutes that seemed more like twenty, he stood up and threw the rock he had brought with him at the spot where he had first seen the thing. The stone hit with a loud splash, and ripples spread out from the impact, but there was still no sign of it.

"Crap," he swore, and went back to his bike. His next stop would be The Logs, but this time he would ride his bike on the path that ran along the river and keep a lookout for the thing. The trip only took a few minutes, and when he reached The Logs, there was still no sign of the creature. *Fine,* he thought, *let's try the beach.*

This ride was shorter and faster than the one from the rocks to The Logs. The ground was flatter and open so he could pedal harder and still see the whole river. It was only twenty yards wide and shallow at this point, so he thought he would see it if it was there.

The beach was just a few years old. The town had cleared a few acres of riverfront, graded the land, and brought in enough sand to cover the ground and the first ten feet or so of the river bottom. The beach side was shallow enough for toddlers. The opposite side faced on the mountain, and it was deep enough to dive into off the rocks that lined it. There was a tree with a rope swing fifty yards downstream for the more adventurous.

Bran was surprised to find a bunch of teenagers, three boys and two girls, swimming there. He stopped to watch them for a few minutes, and then started to move on. He stopped short when one of the girls screamed and disappeared from sight. He froze, and then she reappeared, laughing. The boy who had pulled her under surfaced next to her and grabbed for her again. When one of the boys on the rocks saw him watching them, he yelled, "Hey, kid, beat it," and Bran knew it was time to leave.

It was the same story at the rocks. There was no sign of

the thing, and that was where the path along the shore ended. Now he was forced to take the road that ran thirty yards from the water. He was hoping there would be a ladder or something at the trestle so he could climb up without having to scale fifteen feet of rock wall to reach the iron framework that spanned the river. He could do it, but it was a challenge.

Excellent, Bran thought when he found a wooden pallet stacked up against the stone abutment. He parked his bike, mounted the pallet, and carefully scaled the remaining distance to the top. When he got there, he was rewarded with an unobstructed view up and down the river. Two steel I-beams spanned the space between where he was standing and the opposite bank. The stone support pillar midway across provided an excellent vantage point for looking into the water below without having to balance on the I-beams.

Bran walked the downstream I-beam all the way across to the opposite shore and filled his pockets with rocks. They were plentiful there. The mountain had been blasted to make way for an underground pipeline and provided an inexhaustible supply of rocks that he and Ryan used to toss at fish in the river. When his pockets were full, he made his way back to the middle of the trestle and lined his rocks up so they were easy to get at.

This is boring, he thought after a half-hour of waiting, and then started looking for any convenient target in the river below. His first victim was a rainbow trout that was hovering near the surface in the current. It was waiting for the river to bring it flies and other small tidbits. Bran drew back his arm and let fly with one of his rocks. He knew he had no chance of hitting it, but it was fun to chase it around the river. "Take that," he yelled as each rock hit the water. He was getting ready to throw his last rock when the creature appeared directly below him.

"Damn," he swore, and automatically looked to see if Ryan had heard him. Then he remembered he was alone. The creature was clinging to the stones of the pillar beneath him. Bran wanted to throw his last stone at it, but then decided he'd better hang onto it, so he put it in his pocket instead.

He felt safe where he was even though the thing in the water obviously knew he was there. "Get! Go away," he yelled at it, his heart pounding, but it just stared back up at him with lidless eyes. When it opened its mouth to grin at him, Bran could see wicked-looking pointed teeth.

They were stuck there—Bran on the trestle, the creature just beneath the surface of the river below him. The lidless ice-blue eyes in its reptilian face seemed to call out to him to jump. It had impossibly long, stick-thin arms that ended in wicked-looking claws. He couldn't see the rest of its body, so he moved to the side to get a better look at it. When he did, it mirrored his movement.

"Go away!" he screamed at it, but it stayed where it was, waiting for him to do something. When it didn't move, he took his last rock out of his pocket and threw it as hard as he could at the thing's head.

"Ha!" he yelled when he scored a direct hit on the thing's face. His joy at hitting it only lasted a second because it lifted its head out of the water and hissed at him. It sounded like a snake, only louder, and it chilled him to the bone. *That's it. I'm out of here,* he thought, and headed back across the river toward his bike. This time, though, he straddled the I-beam —he was too nervous to walk it.

The creature followed him as he made the journey back. Now he could see its entire body. It appeared to be at least ten feet long. It had a reptilian head and long, skinny arms. From its chest down it looked like a big snake or eel, with a tail that swished back and forth as it moved through the water. It was swimming on its back, never taking its eyes off him. Its arms trailed along its sides, and its snow-white underside made it look like a giant slug slipping through the water.

"Go away!" he screamed again when he reached the safety of the other abutment. Then he edged himself over the side before dropping to the ground. He was just getting on his bike when the thing lunged out of the river and started to slowly slither toward him. Its claws sunk into the bank as it pulled itself across the ground he had thought would protect him.

"Go away!" he screamed again, and this time he was crying. When the thing lifted itself up on its arms and hissed at him, it broke his paralysis and he started pedaling. He didn't look back until he was twenty yards away. When he did, he was just in time to see its tail slip off the bank and disappear into the river.

Scared and shaken, Bran retreated to their fort where he closed the door and shivered in the dark. *Stupid, stupid, stupid,* he admonished himself, and knew he wasn't going to tell Ryan about what he had done.

Chapter 9

Longo watched Ryan and Bran as they came toward him. Today was the day he was going to talk to them. Ever since last week, they had stopped talking whenever they got within fifty feet of him, and neither one of them would look him in the eye. "Morning, boys. Have you got a minute?" he said when they got to the crossing

They shared the look they had shared when Erickson had approached them before Bran answered. "What for?"

"I was hoping you'd tell me what you saw at The Rock the day that other boy drowned."

"We didn't see anything," Ryan said a little too quickly.

Dave knew it was no use trying to get them to talk if they didn't want to, so he tried a little honey instead of vinegar. "If you tell me what you saw, I'll tell you what it is."

Silence, then the look, and then Ryan said, "We were at The Rock, and Bran saw something in the water. I didn't see it at first, but then he chucked a rock at it and it moved."

"How did it move?"

"It swam toward us underwater," Bran said.

"Did you get a good look at it?"

"Sort of. It was brown, had long arms with claws, and its eyes were bright blue."

Erickson looked at Ryan and asked, "Is that what you saw, too?"

"Yeah," Ryan told him.

"Anything else?" Erickson asked.

The boys looked at each other, and then Ryan said, "No, sir."

Dave looked at the Bran and said, "Okay, why don't you tell me the rest of it."

"We did," Ryan protested, but Bran just stared at his shoes.

"Brandon?" Dave prompted.

"Tell us what it is first," Bran answered.

"It's called an oniare, and I've seen it, too," Dave told him.

"When?"

"Before you were born. It's not something you want to get close to," Dave said to him, and showed him the scars on his leg.

Bran gasped, "Oh man, the creature did that?"

"Uh huh," Longo answered. "Now tell me the rest of it."

Bran looked at Ryan before answering. Then he told them what he had done.

"Are you nuts?" Ryan said when Bran finished. "Why did you do that?"

"You weren't here, and I had nothing else to do, so I just thought I'd try to find it. I never thought it would come after me," Bran told him, trying to justify his actions.

"Well, I think it was pretty stupid," Ryan told him.

"Let's not call it stupid," Longo told them.

"Yeah," Bran agreed, "because now we know for sure there really is a monster in the river—a monster that kills people."

Chapter 10

Summer, 1939

"Jesus, Dave, what the hell happened back there?" Chief Miller asked as they were driving the body to Tom Blakely's funeral home.

Longo looked down at the bloody bandage peeking out from his shredded pant leg. He had wrapped his undershirt around the gashes, but bright red blood was starting to seep through. "How should I know? All I know is John and I saw something in the river. You know everything that happened after that," Longo answered.

"Well, I'll drop you off at Doc Gordon's and then I'll take the body to Tom's. You're going to need some stitches, maybe a lot of stitches," the Chief told him. "Think about what you're going to tell him about how your leg got torn up."

"Right," Dave agreed, wondering how he was going to explain his injury to the doctor.

"And Dave, let's keep what happened to ourselves for now," Miller told him.

* * *

Doc Gordon unwrapped Longo's calf and whistled when he saw the damage. "Those are some pretty nasty cuts you've got there, Dave. How did you do this?"

"Caught it on some barbed wire by the old Mosure Farm," Longo told him. It was the best he could think of on the ride over.

"Really? They look too even for barbed wire. Barbed wire cuts usually look pretty ragged. These are clean and sharp," Gordon observed.

"Nope, barbed wire," Dave insisted.

"Okay, Dave, whatever you say," Gordon replied as he numbed Dave's leg before he started to clean the wounds. By the time he was done with the needle and thread, Longo had over a hundred stitches in his leg, and a tetanus shot in his ass.

"I'd stay off that leg for a while, Dave. The last thing you want to do is pull any of those stitches out. Keep it elevated and come back in a week and we'll see about taking them out. It's going to hurt like a bitch when the Novocain wears off, and you're going to be pretty sore for a while after that. Do you want something for the pain? I could give you some codeine, or even some morphine, if it gets too bad."

"I'll take the codeine," Dave told him.

Gordon gave him the painkillers. "You're going to need a ride, too. There's no way you can drive with that leg. You need me to call someone?"

"You can try the station. The Chief can come for me if he's there."

Gordon left Dave in the waiting room while he made the call to the station. When he came back, he told Dave, "The Chief wasn't there, but my son Roger can drive you when he gets back. It shouldn't be too long."

* * *

"So what killed him?" Chief Miller asked the mortician, who also served as the coroner out here in the boonies.

"He drowned," Blakely answered, "but he didn't go quietly. I've never seen anything like this."

"Like what?" the Chief asked.

"Like this," Blakely answered, "Look at his face. He was terrified. These cuts, they're deep, and they cover his entire body." When Miller took a good look at them, he saw that in some places the white bone of the victim's ribs showed through.

"And look at this. Some of his fingernails are broken, and he has something under the others. This guy fought for his life. You've got a killer out there somewhere. I can do an autopsy, if you want. See if I can find out anything more."

"No need," Miller told him. "We know he drowned and there was a hell of a struggle. I think that's all we need to know. Besides, the town hasn't got the money for an autopsy."

"Maybe the state would pay for it," Blakely said.

"No, let's just leave it where it is. And, I'd sort of like to keep that between you and me for a while." Miller added.

"Why's that?" Blakely wanted to know.

It took a minute for Miller to answer. "I just do. Can we leave it at that for now?"

Blakely shook his head and then reluctantly agreed. "You're the Chief."

"What else can you tell me about him?" Miller asked.

"He's not from town; at least I've never seen him before. How about you?"

"No, I don't think so either, and I know most of the kids living here. Could he be visiting someone?"

64

"Well, small as he is, he's not a kid. I'd say he's in his mid-twenties. His hands are pretty calloused, so he was a working man. His arms and face are really tanned, but the rest of him is as white as snow. I'd say he was an itinerant worker looking for work or just passing through."

"Yeah, I'll have Dave Longo check that out. I'd hate for it to be a local," the Chief told him.

After Miller left, Blakely covered the corpse with a white sheet. Neither of them suspected something was growing within the body. If the loosely draped sheet hadn't been there, they might have seen the corpse's stomach bulge and ripple as if something was moving around inside. It was more like the belly of a pregnant woman close to giving birth than that of a lifeless corpse.

* * *

"Dave, I need you to …" the Chief started to say when Longo came into the station. The words died on his lips when he realized he was walking with the aid of a cane.

"How's the leg?" he asked instead.

"I'll live, but the doc says I have to stay off it for a while."

"Any stitches?"

"Bout' a hundred," Longo responded.

Miller was astonished. "A hundred, are you kidding?"

"Nope. Five gashes, and they were all fairly deep. Took about twenty in each one," Dave explained. "What happened at Blakely's?"

"Tom says the guy drowned, but he was in a hell of a fight before he went down. He also thinks he was in his twenties and might have been a transient. My guess is he rode the train in and went down to the river to wash up before coming into town. I was going to ask you to check that out, but I'll do it myself. You hold down the fort here while I'm gone."

I've got to talk to the mayor about getting another officer, Miller thought as he parked his car and made his way toward the spot where the river ran by the railroad tracks. He knew it wasn't going to happen; money was tight, but he could always try. Hell, he was lucky to have Dave.

The path to the river was strewn with trash blown in by the trains as they passed. Miller hadn't been down there in a while, and he was surprised at the difference time and prosperity had wrought here. In the years after the big crash in '29, a hobo camp had blossomed here. Whole families and lots of transients lived in tin shacks and existed on begged or stolen food. That was all gone now, and the land was reverting back to forest. It was mostly shrubs and a few scattered trees, but in a few years, all signs of the camp would be gone.

When he reached the river, he was less than a half mile from The Rock as the crow flies, but more than a mile walking. The path along the riverbank was still there, and Miller followed it downstream. It was shallow here, less than a few feet deep, but after a hundred yards he came across the pool that people in the camp had used for washing and swimming in the summer months.

What's that? he thought when he spied something on the bank ahead. As he got closer to it, he realized it was a pile of neatly folded clothes set atop a battered cardboard suitcase. An equally battered pair of shoes sat next to it. *Well, this is where he went in,* Miller thought as he bent to examine the clothes. The first thing he found was a worn leather wallet with a single dollar bill and a tattered driver's license with the name Sean McCauley inside it. Other than that, it was empty.

Miller stared at the river, and wondered, *So, Sean McCauley, what happened when you stepped into the water here?* Imagined scenes from McCauley falling and drowning to his being dragged under by the claws that had erupted out of the river and grabbed Longo's leg ran through his head. The hairs on the back of his neck and arms stood on end.

I'm being watched, he thought, and spun around to see if there was anyone there. There wasn't. He started to relax, but then the feeling hit him again, stronger this time. He spun back to the river and caught sight of a snake-like face with ice-blue eyes watching him from the middle of the pool. *What the hell?* It was only there for an instant before it slipped beneath the surface, but it chilled him to the bone.

Chapter 11

May, 2014

Poquonock High School Class of 1964

Dear Classmates,

So far over fifty graduates of the class of '64 have signed up to attend the reunion. I've attached a list below. I've also attached a list of classmates we can't locate. If you know how we can reach any of these missing friends, please let us know.

The Reunion Committee

Ryan scanned the attachment and, sure enough, his name was there on the list of those attending. Most of the girls—women—now had different last names, but their maiden names were included so he could tell who they were. He was disappointed to see that Betty Hainley's name was missing. How many of his classmates, he wondered, had been married and divorced? How many had passed away? How many were still single like him? Most of all, he wondered if he would go. Could he actually bring himself to return to the place that haunted his dreams? He thought he could, but he needed to know about the creature.

* * *

He wasn't a computer wiz, but he was learning. His search for missing persons and mysterious drownings in Poquonock had been impossible at first, but when he finally got the knack of searching the web, a pattern started to emerge. Every fifteen to twenty years, there were three or four people who drowned in the river or who went missing and were never found. Those who drowned were usually found days or weeks later, and in each case, the body had been ravaged by turtles, fish, and eels.

The oniare, it had to be the oniare, he thought. *It's still there, and it's overdue for a return.* Then he realized that the time span between missing persons and Bran's visits were the same. *Jesus, Bran. Are you actually visiting me? Are you trying to tell me the oniare is back?*

Chapter 12

Summer, 1956

"Did you know that Chuck Turcott is an Iroquois Indian?" Longo asked the boys.

"You mean Old Man Turcott?" Ryan asked.

"Yes, Old Man Turcott," Dave answered. "His Indian name is *Watches from the Bank*. Do you want to know why?"

"Yeah," Bran answered, intrigued that there was a real, live Indian living in town, even if it was creepy Old Man Turcott.

"It's because he's responsible for watching for the **oniare**. That's the thing you saw."

"What's an oniare?" Ryan asked.

"Chuck says an Iroquois legend described it as a dragon-like, horned water serpent that lived in the Great Lakes, where it would capsize canoes and eat people. The creature you boys saw in the river is the basis for that legend."

"The Great Lakes? Where are they?" Ryan asked.

"A long way from here, but all the tribes had a legend about it," Longo explained.

"If the lakes are a long way from here, how did it get here?"

Bran demanded.

Smart boy, Longo thought. "I think it came up the river from Lake Champlain."

"How do you know all this?" Bran wanted to know.

"Because Chuck told me about it after I had my first run in with it," Longo answered. He wasn't about to tell them the whole story, just enough to convince them to keep away from the creature. "I'm only telling you this because you've seen the thing. And you," he said, pointing to Bran, "have drawn its attention. It knows who you are, so stay away from the river."

* * *

They did, for almost a week, but it was summer, school was finally out, and there were only so many things to do that didn't involve the river. They worked on their fort, rode bikes, read comics, snuck into the dump to shoot at rats with their slingshots, flipped baseball cards, and played mumblety-peg. Ryan wasn't about to admit it, but even he was getting bored. And then Bran showed up at Ryan's house with a towel and wearing his swim suit.

"We're not going swimming," Ryan insisted. "I'm not going anywhere near the river, and neither are you." Bored was one thing, dead was something else entirely.

"Come on, chicken. I'm not talking about The Rock or the trestle. It's The Back Beach. There'll be lots of people there," Bran told him for what seemed like the umpteenth time.

"Look, let's just ride down there, see if anyone's swimming. Then we can decide whether to go in, or not. Can we at least do that?"

"Fine," Ryan answered, giving in at last. He knew Bran would never stop until he got his way. And let's face it, he missed swimming, too. "Let me get my stuff."

"Cool, let's go," Bran told his friend when Ryan came back in his swim suit. He started peddling before Ryan had even mounted his bike. Then, as usual, Ryan was racing to catch up.

* * *

"See, plenty of people, and the lifeguard can see if any-thing's coming," Bran said in his *I-tolda-you-so* voice. "Now let's hit the water!" Then he was off his bike and running toward the river. "Last one in's a rotten egg," he called as he ran.

Ryan still wasn't sure he wanted to do this, even if there were a lot of people at the beach and the lifeguard was sitting on his tower. In addition to the lifeguard, who was just a teenager, he counted four grownups and at least two dozen kids on this side and another six across the river on the rock ledge. Eventually the draw of the river overcame his fear. Swimming was his favorite thing to do. He couldn't imagine staying out of the water all summer. He finally gave in completely and climbed off his bike when Bran hit the water and started swimming toward the other side. He leaned his bike against a tree because the kickstand was useless in the soft dirt. Then he ran to the water. He hit it at a full run, wanting to reach the other side before Bran could climb far enough up the rocks to cannonball him when he got there.

Man, I'm too late, Ryan thought as he watched Bran climb out of the water and scale the rocks. *Well, we'll just see about that. I'll swim underwater the rest of the way.*

He didn't give Bran a target and easily made the last ten feet underwater. But, when he surfaced and took a gulp of air, all he got was water. Bran had timed it perfectly and hit the water right in front of him when he came up. He gasped, choked, and almost puked, but he wouldn't give Bran the satisfaction of knowing he had scored one on him. "Asshole," he said, and pushed his friend's head under water.

"Let's go to the rope swing," Bran suggested when they were both sitting on the rock ledge, warming themselves in the sun.

"No way! I'm staying here where the people are," Ryan told him.

"Oh, come on, you chicken."

"No!" Ryan blurted out, letting his friend know he was serious. He had only agreed to go swimming because he felt there was safety in numbers. They'd be alone at the rope swing.

"Well, I'm going," Bran told him, and headed for the path along the river that led to the swing and the jumping tree. It was only fifty yards downstream, and he was there in a matter of minutes.

* * *

When he reached the tree, Bran turned to make sure Ryan had followed him. He was shocked when he found the path empty. *He's really not coming,* he thought. He almost turned around and went back, but then his stubborn streak kicked in.

Fine. I'll do it by myself, he thought as he looked for the rope. It should have been tied to the jumping tree, but it wasn't. Instead, it was hanging over the water about five feet from shore. He had two choices, he could wade out and get it … boring, or he could climb the twenty feet to the plank nailed to a crotch between two branches of the tree and jump the twenty-five feet to the river below. Jumping was definitely the way to go.

Boards had been nailed to the tree to form a sort of ladder up to the jumping-off spot. They had been put there by the older kids, so they were a bit far apart for him, but he managed.

When he got to the jumping platform, he stood there for a moment admiring the view up and down the river. He looked back along the path to see if Ryan was coming, but it was still empty.

The heck with him, Bran thought. Directly below him was a rock shelf and the water was only a foot or so deep. Ten feet from shore, there was a sheer drop off. It was over ten feet deep there. The tree extended five feet over the water, so he had to make sure he jumped far enough to clear the ledge.

He leaned forward and was prepared to yell *"Geronimo,"* and leap out into space when he saw movement in the water below. "Whoa!" he yelled, and grabbed the tree's trunk to keep from falling. When he managed to steady himself, he looked down to see the horrendous face of the **oniare**. It was staring back up at him … waiting for him to jump.

Fuck you, Bran thought. There was no way he was jumping, and that meant he was going to have to climb back down, and that wasn't going to be easy. The steps were too far apart for going down.

He got down the first two steps before looking down. He froze when he saw the creature just starting to drag itself out of the water. It was going to be a race to see who got to the bottom of the tree first. He tried to hurry, and in his haste, almost missed the next step. *Slow down, slow down,* he told himself, but the creature was already completely out of the water. Another step for him, another foot for the creature. He heard the scrape of its claws on stone and the slap of its tail as it struggled to get to the base of the tree before him. He was terrified he wasn't going to make it. He might have to jump when he got closer to the ground. He was at the last step when he realized he was going to lose the race. Those claws that had made such terrible noises as they scraped across stone were going to rip him apart.

He started to scramble back up the tree and then a scream broke the silence. "Aaarrrrgh!" And there was Ryan, beating at the creature with a branch he had found along the path. "Jump," he yelled when the thing turned its attention to him. Bran reacted immediately. He leapt off the tree, just clearing the oniare's grasp. Then both boys were running back toward the beach and what they hoped was the safety of numbers.

Chapter 13

May, 2014

Ryan paused. All he had to do was left click and Google Earth would take him to Poquonock. Just one click. His finger hesitated, and then … he did it. The earth rotated and expanded before his eyes and in less than a second it was taking him to upstate Vermont and zooming in on the town that he hadn't seen since his high school graduation in 1964.

There it is. I wonder how much it's changed.

The first difference he noticed was that there was a four-lane highway running across the south end of town. *Where the hell did that come from?*

As he scrolled over the town, it finally hit him that the Poquonock he remembered was gone. Well, partly gone at least; the river was still there. Using his mouse, he clicked and dragged his way along its path.

He started at the dam, where he got his first surprise. Just down from the spillway, after the river passed under Main Street, the old railroad trestle was missing. The right of way was still there, but even the tracks appeared to be gone. He paused in his exploration as nostalgia tore at him, threatening to end his search. His mind drifted, and he found himself back on the trestle with Bran, clinging to a steel girder as the train thundered down on them.

* * *

"We have to get off and run as soon as it passes," Bran called out to him over the roar of the approaching engine.

"I know," he shouted back as the trestle began to vibrate. At first, it was nothing more than a slight tremble; then, as the train drew closer, the tremble intensified. When the engine's wheels rolled onto the trestle, the entire structure started to shake. Ryan felt it in his body and he yelled in joy as adrenalin pumped through his blood. And then the train was thundering by: first, the engine, and then three passenger cars. Now the trestle was shaking so hard it felt like it would toss him off like a leaf blown from a tree in a strong wind if he was foolish enough to loosen his grip. As it sped past he could see the faces of the riders, and from the look of surprise on their faces, at least a couple of them saw him, too.

He was still clinging to the girder when Bran shouted at him. "Let's go! We have to be out of here if the cops come."

"Right," he answered, but there was so much adrenaline pumping through him that he was still shaking. He had to take a minute to calm down before he could trust himself to make his way back to the track, and then off the trestle.

"Let's go, let's go," Bran called to him as Ryan carefully stepped from tie to tie. He could see the river below in the gaps between them. It was shallow there, no more than four feet deep, and he could see several trout, brookies probably … or maybe rainbows, hanging in the current. One misstep and his leg could slip between the ties and he could be stuck there like a beetle on a pin. Then he was off the trestle and they were sliding down the embankment in a shower of small stones as they sought the safety of the woods.

"Here they come," Bran said as they watched a police car with its lights flashing pull up and stop on the Main Street Bridge.

The cop got out and scanned the trestle. Ryan knew they were invisible hiding in the trees, but the fear of discovery was enough to get his heart racing again.

"Man, we've got ..." and then the memory faded and he was back at his laptop, staring at the screen.

* * *

He mentally shook himself and continued moving his mouse along the river's path. It played hide and seek as it passed beneath a green canopy of trees, mostly oak and maple, he remembered. It made a big, sweeping loop out before slipping back toward Main Street. Then, after a short, straight run there, it cut left and practically disappeared as it made its way toward The Rock. If he hadn't known where to look, he might have lost it. Then it burst back into view, and there it was, The Rock, nothing more than a small, gray splotch on the screen from this altitude.

The imagery date on the Google Earth screen was 6/17/2010, almost fifty-four years to the day since he and Bran had first seen the thing in the river.

Chapter 14

Summer, 1939

When Chief Miller came back to the station, Dave could tell something was wrong. "What happened?" he asked as Miller sank into the chair behind the old, wooden desk that had been there longer than either of them.

"I saw it. The thing in the river," Miller told him.

"You saw it. Jesus, what is it?" Longo shot back at him, wincing as he took his injured leg off of his own desk and sitting bolt upright.

"It's like nothing I've ever seen before, like nothing I could have imagined. It's not human, I can tell you that, or like any animal I've ever heard of."

Longo waited, but the Chief just sat there in silence, not saying anything more. Dave waited as long as he could before prompting, "Go on."

"I found McCauley's clothes—that's his name, Sean Mc-Cauley—neatly folded on the bank, down where the squatters used to bathe in the river. I was looking through his wallet when I knew, just knew, someone—something—was watching me. I didn't see anyone until I spun around and got a glimpse of it in the river. It was only there for a second or two, but it scared the shit out of me. I didn't even walk the bank to look for it. I just grabbed McCauley's stuff and got the hell out of there."

"What did it look like?" Longo asked.

"All I saw was a snake-like face. It had ice-blue eyes, not just the iris, but the entire eye. I didn't see a nose, I don't think it has one, but its mouth was huge, and filled with wicked-looking teeth. It was there, and then it was gone," Miller told him.

"Damn," Dave swore. "I never saw what clawed my leg, but from the cuts, and the way it grabbed me, it must have a five-fingered hand. What the hell can it be?"

* * *

When Charles "Chuck" Turcott walked into the office two days later, Miller and Longo still had no idea what the creature was, or where it had come from.

"Afternoon, Chief; afternoon, Dave. There's some pretty wild rumors floatin' around town about some kind of creature in the river."

"Where'd you hear that?" the chief asked.

"Oh, around, I don't need to be saying any names. Besides, that's not why I'm here."

"Then why are you here?" Miller asked.

Turcott ignored the question. "I also heard that Dave over there," he nodded in Longo's direction, "had a little accident with some barbed wire."

"Yeah, so?" Miller said.

"Well, I'd like to see those gashes on Dave's leg—if I could," Turcott told them.

"Why?" Miller demanded.

"Because if they look like claw marks, I might know what your creature is."

Miller looked at Longo and nodded, "Go ahead, Dave. Let's see what he has to say."

Longo rolled up his pant leg and started to unwrap the gauze bandages. The deeper he got into the bandage, the more blood staining there was.

"I'm guessing you've got four or five long, deep cuts on that leg, Dave. The kind of cuts a sharp knife ... or claws might make."

Longo paused and stared at Turcott for a minute before taking the bandage off completely. The wounds looked a lot better today than they had two days ago. The swelling was gone, and so was the redness from around the edges. Dark, thin scabs had formed where the cuts were healing back together. Along with the black thread of the stitches, they looked like five little train tracks running along Longo's calf.

"Put it up here on the desk," Turcott said, and when Dave did, he spread his hand over the wounds, each finger just above one of the slashes.

"It grabbed you like this, and then dragged its claws down your leg like this," Turcott told him as he ran his fingers just above the five rows of stitches. "You were damn lucky to get away, you know."

"You mean you actually know what this thing is?" the Chief asked.

"I do. It's an oniare," Turcott told them.

"What the hell is an oniare?" Longo demanded.

"The oniare are an old race. They were here before the white man, they were here before the red man. Maybe they've always been here. We speak of them in our legends," Turcott told him.

"*We?* Who are *we?*" Miller asked.

"We, the Iroquois. The original people of this land," Turcott answered.

"You're Iroquois? I never knew that," Miller said.

"Not too many do. Not too many care."

"So, tell us about this *oniare*," Longo said.

"I called it oniare because it's the easiest to pronounce. To the Iroquois it is oniare. The Algonquian call it the *mishiginebig*. I don't know what others call it. It was said to be a horned serpent that lives in lakes and rivers. It was also said that it kills and eats people. That's what killed that man and attacked Dave," Turcott told them.

"You're not serious," Miller responded, "A horned serpent that kills and eats people?"

"I'm deadly serious. My father told me about it when I was a boy. He died fighting an oniare. It ripped him apart. That's when I became *Watches from the Bank.* My task is to watch for the oniare. Now another one has returned, and I must find it, and kill it—if I can."

"And if you can't?" Miller asked.

"Then it will kill me, and one of you will have to kill it," Turcott told them.

Chapter 15

The boys raced back to the beach. It wasn't until they got there that they realized they still had a big problem.

"How are we going to get to the other side?" Ryan asked as they stood on the rock ledge across from the beach.

Bran glanced nervously up and down the river before answering. "We could swim, or we can walk up to The Logs and cross there."

Ryan looked at him as if he was crazy. "Swim! Are you nuts? That thing is right there in the river."

"Yeah, but it only came after me when I was alone. I think we're safe with all these people here. If we go to The Logs, we'll be alone again," Bran reasoned.

"I don't know," Ryan told him. "If it catches us in the water, we're dead."

Bran thought about this and had to agree. "So what are we going to do, wait here all day?"

Ryan shrugged his shoulders and stared at the water. "I

don't know," he confessed. Twenty minutes later they were still there: it was the longest Bran had sat still since school let out for the summer.

"It's gotta be gone," Bran said, and looked to Ryan for confirmation.

"And what if it's not? What if it's just waiting for you? What if it's after me now because I hit it with that stick?"

Bran sat and fidgeted, and Ryan knew he wouldn't last much longer. "We have to do something, and I'm tired of just sitting here. If it was here, it would have grabbed one of them," Bran said, pointing at the older kids that were treading water and dive bombing each other from The Rock. "I'm going," he finally said, and dove off The Rock. He swam like a madman until he reached the other shore. Then he turned around and called back to Ryan. "Come on, chicken!"

"Man," Ryan mumbled under his breath, and launched himself off the ledge in a shallow dive that would keep him near the surface. Too late, he thought he saw something in the river, a face staring up at him from the bottom. He hit the water with his eyes closed and came up swimming as fast as he could, his heart pumping wildly, praying he'd make it to the other side. When he reached it, he turned back in time to see a teenager's grinning head break the surface just before one of his friends cannonballed him.

"See, I told you," Bran said as Ryan stood doubled over, panting on the beach.

Ryan didn't answer, and he shrugged his friend's hand off when Bran put it on his shoulder. Then he turned and walked away.

"Where are you going? Ryan, where are you going?" Bran called after him as Ryan got on his bike.

"Home," Ryan told him as he started pedaling. Bran called to him again, but Ryan never looked back.

* * *

The next morning Bran was sitting in front of the fort, throwing his hunting knife at a log, when Ryan came up on him from behind. He actually jumped when Ryan said, "Don't you ever do something like that again. If you do, I'm not going to be your friend anymore."

"It was kind of stupid, wasn't it?"

"Yeah, well ... you've had a bad case of the stupids ever since we saw that thing."

"Yeah," Bran agreed, but he wouldn't meet his friend's eyes. Instead, he threw his knife into the log again.

"Why did you do it? You know what Mister Longo said. Bran, you have to stay away from the river."

Bran fingered his knife, and finally said, "I can't."

"What? Why not?" Ryan demanded.

"Because the commies killed my Dad in Korea so I could be safe. I can't let that thing scare me away from the river," Bran told him, and this time threw the knife so hard it buried itself an inch into the log; he had to yank really hard to get it out.

* * *

Bran had been thinking about his dad all day. He didn't remember him, but he knew what he looked like from the pictures in the family album. There was a big picture of him on his mom's dresser, and there was a box in the living room with the American flag and the medals he had won—but at the end of the day, there was no dad to hug him goodnight or take him fishing on weekends. Sometimes Bran hated him for not being there—but mostly he missed him.

"Oh," was all Ryan could say. Then, after a bit, he added, "But we don't have to go looking for trouble; we don't have to go to the river every day, do we?"

"No, but I'm not running from it either, not while I have my Dad's knife," Bran told him, and once again stuck the blade deep into the log he had been using for target practice.

Chapter 16

Summer, 1939

Captain Miller and Dave Longo were sitting in the station trying to decide how they were going to deal with the oniare. Miller was all for letting Turcott deal with it by himself. Longo, on the other hand, thought they should team up with the man.

"He's the one who knows what this thing is. He knows how to kill it. Let's just let him do it," Miller argued.

"And what if it kills him? Then we'll have to go after it, and we'll have no idea what we're doing. That scares the hell out of me," Longo told him.

Miller was about to answer when they heard the door open. All talk of the oniare was put on hold as Tom Blakely walked into the station.

"Morning, Tom, what can I do for you?" Miller asked.

"What do you want me to do with McCauley's body, Chief? I've got to embalm him, or bury him, it's up to you. Either way, the town's going to have to pay for it. I can't afford to eat that loss."

"Let's bury him," Miller replied. "And nothing fancy, a cheap pine box and that's it. Send a bill, the town can take care of that. If anyone comes to claim him, we can always dig him back up."

"Okay," Blakely agreed. "I'll send you the bill when it's done."

Once he was gone, the chief turned to Longo. "Okay, Dave, you're right. If the oniare kills him, we're left to deal with it on our own. We'll work with Chuck to get rid of this thing."

* * *

Blakely didn't have a pine box. There was no money to be made in them. Not too many folks wanted them these days, maybe because it reminded them too much of the depression. But the Chief said keep it cheap, so he had Buddy Jordan make one. Buddy was a jack of all trades and would do just about anything, from making a pine box to digging a grave, to make a buck.

"This deep enough for you, Tom?" Buddy asked as he threw another shovel-full of earth out of the hole he was in. There had been no service for **Sean McCauley**, and there were no mourners here for the burial. They were alone in the cemetery.

"Yes, that should do it," Blakely answered. "Let's get him down there and cover him up."

"Got it," Buddy answered, and tossed the shovel out of the hole. "Give me a hand out of here, and then I'm going to need some help with the ropes."

As Buddy arranged the ropes to lower the casket into the grave, he thought he heard noises coming from inside the box … like the guy inside was scratching on the lid. *Scratch …* *scratch …* and then silence. "What the hell?" he cried, jumping back, crossing himself and letting the coffin drop the last two feet to the bottom of the grave. Luckily, it didn't split open.

"What?" Blakely asked, surprised at Buddy's actions.

"I heard something inside the box. What the hell? Is that guy still alive in there?"

Blakely laughed. "Don't worry, Buddy, he's dead. It was probably just gas. Corpses do that. Sometimes it sounds like a fart, sometimes it sounds like they're moaning. I actually saw one corpse sit up. It scared the hell out of me, too, the first time I saw it."

Buddy looked warily at the coffin, but trusted Blakely's explanation. "If you say so, Tom, but that's really creepy."

* * *

The box was in the ground, and Buddy was shoveling dirt back into the hole when a low noise, like escaping air, came from it. Even if the sound of earth hitting the wooden lid hadn't drowned it out, it would probably have been too low to be heard from where he was standing. Inside the coffin, the young oniare had just ripped its way out of Sean McCauley. It had consumed all the internal organs, and now it was time for it to leave … time to make its way to a deep, protective lake where it could grow to maturity.

It should have emerged into cool, welcoming water; instead, it found itself in warm, fetid air. It hissed in the dark and struggled to escape the confines of the coffin. When it couldn't, it burrowed back into McCauley's body, seeking safety. Eventually, it would die there.

Chapter 17

Summer, 1956

"Maybe we can kill it," Bran said as they sat in the fort.

"Man, I thought we weren't going to talk about that thing today. I want one day where we just have fun," Ryan said. "And besides, we're just kids. How can we kill something like that?"

Bran didn't answer right away; he just kept throwing his knife into the log. When he did answer, he said, "Fine, so, what do you want to do?" Ryan could tell he wasn't happy about it.

"Let's go look for bottle caps. Maybe we can find some that aren't bent too bad. Last time I found a Schaeffer cap that was almost perfect."

Oh, man, bottle caps, Bran thought. *I want to kill that thing, and he wants to collect bottle caps.* His friend was a collector—bottle caps, matchbook covers, baseball cards, he'd collect anything. One year he collected two pails of acorns, for Pete's sake. Then he had an idea. "Let's go then if we're gonna look for bottle caps," he said, and as usual was first out of the fort, leaving Ryan to close the door. And that meant he was on his bike and pedaling toward The Back Beach before Ryan could object.

"Wait, Bran, wait! Where are you going?" Ryan was yelling. Bran knew he would follow him so he slowed down so his friend could catch up.

Ryan was breathing hard when he finally pulled alongside his friend. Bran didn't give him a chance to object to where he was taking them. "The best caps are at the picnic tables next to the ball field, and we haven't looked there in weeks."

"Okay, but we stay away from the river," Ryan said once he caught his breath. Fifty yards was still too close for comfort, he thought, but as long as they didn't get any closer he was okay with it.

As usual, Bran just dropped his bike when he got off while Ryan took the time to balance his on its kickstand and glance nervously at the river. That meant Bran was already peering over the ground looking for discarded bottle caps before Ryan could join him. He found a red Coke cap, picked it up, put it between his thumb and forefinger, yelled, "Heads up," and flipped it at Ryan, who easily caught it.

"Ah, it's just a Coke, I've got a bunch of these," Ryan said, but he stuck it in his pocket anyway.

"So let's find something better," Bran said as he got down on his hands and knees to crawl under a picnic table.

"Got a Yoo-Hoo and a Nehi orange soda," he called, congratulating himself because he had already found three and Ryan was still looking for his first.

"Hey, I've got a new one. I've never seen it before. Come look," Ryan called. "It's in pretty good shape, too," Ryan said as he handed it over.

Bran took it and had to admit he didn't know what it was either. The background was blue with a squiggly line around the outside. There was a white horse's head with Premium written above it, and Beer below it. "We can take it to Larry's

Liquor Store and see if he can tell us what it is," he suggested.

"Good idea," Ryan said, and stuffed it in his pocket along with the others he had found.

After twenty minutes of searching, they had five Coke caps, two Yoo-hoos, the Nehi, three of the horse head caps, and one Pepsi Cola. They were about to quit when Ryan found the holy grail of bottle caps that he had been looking for forever. "Hey!" he shouted. "Look, I found a White Rock Black Cherry cap."

White Rock caps were hard to find, and even Bran had to admit they were cool. They had a fairy that looked a lot like Tinker Bell on the cap. She was kneeling on a rock, looking into the water, and if you looked real close, you could almost see her boobs.

"Let's see," Bran said, holding out his hand.

Ryan passed him the cap face down, and Bran flipped it over to get a good look at the fairy. But instead of a fairy sitting on the rock, Bran thought he saw the creature staring back at him. "No!" he cried out and dropped it like he had been burned.

"What, did it cut you?" Ryan asked.

"No," Bran told him as he picked it up and looked at it again. This time, the fairy was there in her flimsy outfit, peering into the water. He quickly handed it back to Ryan. He knew it had just been his imagination, but he had no desire to chance seeing the creature again.

"Hey, let's see if we can find out what the horse-head cap is," Ryan said as he hopped on his bike.

"Sure," Bran agreed. Right now he'd agree to anything that took them away from the river and out of the woods. Seeing that thing on the bottle cap had really shaken him up.

Chapter 18

May, 2014

Ryan let the view on Google Earth hover over The Rock before zooming in to get a better look at it. As he spun the wheel on the mouse, his heart was pounding so hard he could feel it beating in his ears as the image expanded on the screen. He brought it all the way down to two hundred feet before he stopped. As he did, the air around him seemed to chill and something flickered in his peripheral vision, but he was too absorbed in the image on the screen to glance over at it. It was the scene of a thousand nightmares, and from what he could see, it hadn't changed all that much. The river still opened up into a wide pool and was forced to turn left when it butted up against The Rock's worn, granite face. If anything, the pool was larger now. The dirt road leading to it from the old gravel pit, and the road from The Rock to The Logs, appeared to be gone.

Downstream, The Logs were also a thing of the past, and there appeared to be a small island in their place. The changes didn't stop there. The baseball field was gone—well, not exactly gone, but it was entirely different. There was a whole sports complex there now. When he zoomed in on it, he found two baseball fields, one of which was also a soccer field. There were also four tennis courts and what appeared to be a building that probably contained restrooms. There was even a paved parking lot with actual painted lines for the spaces. It was a far cry from the ill-kept field that had been there when he was a kid.

Then he noticed The Back Beach was gone. There was just a wide lane through the trees leading down to where it used to be. What the hell? Back in the day that had been the only place where kids in town could swim. Why had they let it revert back to woods? Then his breath stuck in his throat and he thought—*the thing in the river, the oniare, could it still be there?* No, that was impossible, wasn't it? Hadn't Mr. Longo killed it?

Chapter 19

Summer, 1939

The Chief, Longo, and Turcott were gathered at the station to discuss just how Turcott intended to go about killing the thing in the river.

"You're going to kill this—oniare?" the Chief asked.

"Yes," Turcott answered.

"And just how do plan on doing this?" Longo asked.

"My dad said you had to do it with iron," Turcott told him. "That was one thing he swore was true—it must be killed with iron. I'm not sure I believe that, but better safe than sorry. I'm going to find it, lure it from the river, and then kill it with iron."

"Lure it from the river? How the hell do you intend to do that?" Longo asked.

"By using one of you for bait," Turcott told him.

Before either the Chief or Longo could answer, the phone on the Chief's desk rang.

"Miller," he said into the mouthpiece. He listened for a

minute, and then the look on his face darkened.

"When was the last time you saw him?" the Chief asked. He listened for another minute, and then said, "I'll be right over."

"What's wrong?" Longo asked.

"Aaron Billings, Bob Billings' kid, is missing. He went out last night and never came home this morning. Bob called his friends and finally got them to admit they had been drinking down by that old trestle that crosses the river."

"I'll go take a look," Longo said, and started to get up.

"Forget it, Dave. Stay here and hold down the fort until the stitches come out. I'll go check it out," Miller told him. Then he looked at Turcott and said, "You wanna' come, Chuck?"

"Hell, yes," Turcott answered. "But we should stop at my house on the way. I have some things we might need."

* * *

The Chief waited while Turcott retrieved a three-pronged, iron-tipped spear and a machete from his garage. The shaft and blade of the machete were dark and pitted with age, but the machete's edge had the shine of newly sharpened metal. Miller had no doubt it was razor sharp.

"What the hell is that thing?" Miller said as Turcott maneuvered the spear into the car.

"It's a fishing spear. The prongs have barbs that grip the fish like hooks so it can't get away," Turcott told him.

"Okay, I give up. Why do we need that?" Miller asked.

"To drag the oniare from the water. Once we have it on land, it should be easier to kill," Turcott told him. "That's what the machete is for. The prongs and the machete are both made of iron."

"And your dad told you all this?" Miller asked.

"Yes, it's an oral tradition, handed down from father to son. My father told me, and I'll tell my son when I have one."

"Why iron?" Miller asked.

"It's part of the legend. Like I said, I don't know if it's true, but I wouldn't want to take a chance it isn't. Would you?"

Miller patted his revolver and said, "I'm willing to try lead."

They rode the rest of the way in silence, each man thinking about what they would do if they found the creature.

The Chief did his best to avoid the worst of the ruts and humps in the road as they made their way to the old trestle. At a couple of points the road narrowed so much that branches scraped along the sides of the car. "Ah, shit," Miller said as he rounded a corner and saw Aaron's 1934 Plymouth, two-door coupe parked in front of the path leading to the trestle.

"Well, let's take a look," Miller said as he got out of the car.

"Hang on a second, Chief," Turcott said as he maneuvered the fishing spear out of the back seat. "Just in case, ya know?"

Miller didn't say anything; he just nodded and walked toward the river. As soon as they reached the trestle, it was obvious that someone had been partying there. The ground in front of the stone abutment was littered with three un-broken, clear glass pint bottles and glass shards from several amber beer bottles. "Assholes," Turcott said when he saw the mess.

While Miller was checking the ground around the broken beer bottles, Turcott went to the river. "Over here, Chief," he called from the bank beyond the abutment.

Miller joined Turcott where he was standing at the bank and immediately saw gouges torn in the hard-packed earth leading to the river. Where the bank softened to wet clay, there were signs that something heavy had been dragged through it.

While the Chief examined the bank, Turcott used the

grooves and cracks between the stones in the abutment's face to climb the fifteen feet to the top. "Chief, pass me the spear. I'm going to go out to the middle and see if I can see anything."

"Wait, I'll come with you," Miller called back, but when he tried to climb the abutment like Turcott had, he had to admit he couldn't do it. He'd never been good at rock climbing. He looked around for something he could stand on, but couldn't find anything. Instead, he walked around to the bank and watched Turcott, spear in hand, quickly walk the I-beam to the abutment in the center of the span.

"See anything?" he called as Turcott scanned the river.

"No, Chief. Whatever was here is gone," Turcott answered.

* * *

The oniare had been drawn to the men by the noise they made throwing empty bottles into the water and the light from their fire. It had watched from the river, hidden by the darkness, waiting for a chance to seize one of them. It required a host for the life that was growing inside its body. If it didn't find one soon, the fetus would begin to devour the oniare itself for the nourishment it required.

The oniare stayed in the shallows, waiting for one of the men to approach the water. When one did, it would grab the man, drag him into the river, kill him, and transfer the fetus to him. Then it could return to the deep lake that was its home to live out the rest of its life. It would only give birth once in its lifetime. The fetus growing inside it was the second of the three it carried. If this one were lost, it would only have one chance left to continue the species.

As the light from the men's fire diminished, so did the sounds coming from the bank. The men were leaving. It wouldn't find a host this night. But then a single man approached the water. The oniare swam closer as the man stood on the bank and started to urinate into the river. When it was close enough, it launched itself at him, grasped him with its claws, and dragged him into the water. It was all over in less than a minute.

The host struggled, but it was useless. As soon as it opened its mouth to scream, the oniare opened its jaws, placed them over the man's, and prepared to let the fetus make its way up its throat and into the host. It could feel the fetus passing from itself to the host when the man vomited. There was poison in the vomit. It could taste it, bitter and repellent. It jerked its face away from the man's open jaws, trying to block the fetus' path to the poisoned host. But it was too late; it was already gone and clawing its way into the dying man's body.

* * *

Now the oniare watched the man walk across the iron beam that spanned the river. It was hiding in the shadows cast by a tree that overhung the bank. With its coloring, it was difficult to see from only a few feet away, impossible to spot from where the man was.

It still had a single fetus inside its body. It needed another host, and soon, but it was not willing to attack the man on the ground when the one on the trestle could come to his aid. One of its children had been stolen from it, dragged from the river before it could break free from the host. And the second had surely died in its poison-filled host from the night before.

The oniare was becoming desperate; it needed another host. Anything big enough would do. A deer, or a human, would be best. A large dog or a raccoon would be a last resort, but they had claws and teeth. It would avoid those if it could. But soon … it had to find another host soon, before the fetus it carried started to feed on it.

Chapter 20

Summer, 1956

Chief Miller looked up from his desk when Dave Longo walked into the station. School was out for the summer, and since becoming a part-timer, Longo didn't have a lot to do other than putter around in the garden and wait for September. Most summers, that was fine. This summer, however, the garden was the last thing on his mind. The oniare was back, and people were going to die. Dave hadn't been down to the river in years, and it was the last thing he wanted to do now, but sometimes you don't get to do what you want to do—you have to do what you need to do. It had taken him over a week of soul searching to decide to come in and talk to the chief about it. He had never really gotten over the last time, but once the decision was made, he felt the need to get started. Because if he didn't, and a kid died, he'd never forgive himself.

"Dave, I was hoping I'd be seeing you in here. I guess Erickson told you ... the oniare is back," Miller said.

"Yeah, what are you going to do about it?"

"I'm working on that," the chief answered, but Longo could see that he had no idea what he was going to do. He and Turcott and taken care of the last one. "You got any ideas?" he asked Longo.

Longo looked the chief in the eye and knew he wasn't going to like what he said. "You need to patrol the river. Get some volunteers and kill this thing for once and for all."

"How do we do that? I thought you and Turcott killed the damn thing back in '39," Miller said.

"We did. We killed it and burned the body. This has to be a different one," he added.

"Jesus, I was afraid of that. How many of those goddamned things can there be?"

"Don't know," Dave told him, "but we've got another one, and we need to kill it—and sooner would be better than later."

"So what do we do now?" Miller asked. "You must have some ideas since you came in."

Longo looked down, stared at his hands. "Like I said, you need to patrol the river. You need to kill this thing. I thought about asking Chuck Turcott to help, but he's getting a bit old for this. He must be seventy by now, and I don't think he can handle another one. The last one cost him too much. I'd never ask him to do it again. It's gonna have to be me and anybody else you want to cut in on this."

"What happened the last time?" Miller asked.

Dave looked at him, shook his head. "Nope, that's not my story to tell. You want to know that, you ask Chuck."

"I guess I don't need to know. That was then, this is now. You sure you're up to this, Dave?" Miller asked next.

"No, but it's got to be done. I'm the only one with first-hand knowledge of this thing and what it can do. You can count Erickson in because he already knows it's back. You should also put the river off limits until we find it so it doesn't kill anyone else."

The chief shook his head before answering. "How the hell can I put the river off limits? Too many people use it."

"I don't know," Longo answered. "Maybe say there was a chemical spill, or something from the paper mill got in it."

Miller thought about it for a minute and finally said, "I can't do that. If I did, every town downstream would be on my ass to know what it was, and the mill would be all over me. I think we're just going to have to keep this quiet and hope you, me, and Erickson can find this thing."

"Okay," Longo agreed, "but nobody patrols alone."

"Fine," Miller answered. "We'll start tomorrow. I need to talk to Erickson and change some shift coverage, and we don't do it in uniform. People see us down there in uniform and everyone will be asking questions."

"Tell him to meet me at The Rock at seven," Longo said before he left.

* * *

Longo arrived at The Rock at six. He had no intent of going near the water by himself, but he needed some time to think about what he was doing. He hadn't gone near the river since he and Turcott had killed the first oniare. Back in the day, he had been young and fearless … and in shape. Now he was old and fat. *Can I really do this—again?*

As he sat at the top of The Rock, he was surprised at how much it hadn't changed since '39. The tree McCauley had been stuck in was gone, of course, but everything else was pretty much unchanged. Dave stared at the water and felt a chill run up his back. This early in the morning the angle of the sun hitting the water made every ripple sparkle and shine with reflected light. *The damn thing could be right down there looking back at me, and it would be impossible for me to see it.*

The crunch of tires on gravel alerted Longo to Erickson's arrival. Dave glanced at his watch and saw that Erickson was also early; it was only six-thirty. He didn't turn around when he heard the car door close; he just waited for Erickson to join him at the top of The Rock.

"Morning, Dave," Erickson said as he climbed up to meet Longo.

"Morning, Marty," Dave answered.

"How long you been here?" Erickson asked.

"Not long. I just needed some time to think. I haven't been down here since '39."

Erickson sat down beside him and said, "Tell me about this thing, Dave. What is it, and how do we kill it?"

"Chuck Turcott told us everything we know about it, and he helped kill the last one. The Iroquois and the Delaware call it oniare. To the Algonquian it's mishiginebig," Dave answered, stumbling over the last two names. "The only one I can pronounce is oniare, so that's what I call it."

"Yeah, but what the hell is it?" Erickson asked again.

"Chuck said it's part of an old race that was here even before the Indians. The legends say it's a horned water serpent that kills and eats its victims. It's supposed to live in deep lakes."

"Then what's it doing here in the river?"

"I don't know for sure, but I've had a long time to think about it, and I think it might be spawning, like salmon coming back to the river they were born in," Longo told him.

They sat in silence for a while, and then Longo said, "This is where I got those scars on my leg—right here. There was a body caught in the branches of a tree that had fallen into the river. The tree's gone, of course, but it was right down there," he said, pointing to a spot just downstream from where The Rock ended and the dirt path started.

"Fella named John Weiss found it. He saw something in the water that scared him. I saw it, too, but we still had to get the body out of the water, so Chief Miller and I came down here to get it. We almost had it out when a clawed hand came out of the water and grabbed me by the leg. I think it would have dragged me in if the Chief hadn't pulled me to shore. That was the start of it," Longo said as he reached into the cloth sack sitting next to him for a stone.

"What's that for?" Erickson asked.

"The noise attracts it," Longo said, and tossed the stone out into the river. "The problem is, the thing could be down there right now, watching us, and we'd never know it."

Erickson looked at the river and shivered. If this thing, this oniare, was as nasty as Longo made it out to be, he really wanted no part of it.

* * *

"What is it with you and this thing?" Ryan demanded as they sat in the confines of the fort. "Why can't we just stay away from the river like Old Man Turcott told us to?"

"I just can't," Bran answered.

"Why not?"

Bran fiddled with his hunting knife before answering, "I told you, my dad wouldn't run away. My dad didn't run away in Korea."

"Yeah, but your dad got killed in Korea," Ryan said, before thinking.

"Yeah, but he didn't run away, so I can't run away either."

Ryan stared at his hands for a minute and then answered, "Fine, I just hope it doesn't kill us."

"It won't," Bran answered with the certainty of youth.

They sat in silence for a while, and then Ryan asked, "So what's your plan?"

"We're going hunting. I'm going to bring my knife and slingshot, and you're going to bring your bow. Do you think you can get some of your dad's hunting arrows?"

"Maybe … yeah, I guess I can," Ryan told him.

"Could you get the .22?" Bran asked, referring to the single-shot, bolt-action, Savage .22 caliber rifle Ryan and his dad used for target shooting.

"No, he keeps the guns locked up," Ryan answered.

* * *

"Did you get the arrows?" Bran wanted to know when he met Ryan at his house the next morning.

"Shut up!" Ryan hissed. "My mom will kill me if she hears you." They didn't have to worry about his dad because he was a long-haul trucker and was gone for the week. He wouldn't be home until Friday night.

"So where are they?" Bran demanded when they left the house.

"In the shed. I snuck them out last night when my mom was on the phone with my aunt."

When Ryan opened the shed, Bran was amazed at the assortment of stuff stored in there. There was a motor-driven lawn mower, all sorts of shovels and other gardening tools, a Coleman lantern, and, the thing that really drew his attention, a hatchet with a leather cover protecting the head. "Take that, too," he told Ryan, pointing to it.

Ryan nodded, reached out, and took it off the pegs it was mounted on and handed it to Bran. There were slits in the back of the leather cover, so he undid his belt, slipped it through the slits, and hung it off his hip.

When they walked out of Ryan's yard and into the woods, they were armed with Bran's knife and Wham-O slingshot, and Ryan's bow and arrows and the hatchet.

"You got any ammo for that?" Ryan asked, nodding at the slingshot.

"Yeah," Bran answered, and showed his friend a leather bag full of marbles. They wouldn't kill anything bigger than a chipmunk, but they could do some damage, especially if he could hit the thing in the eye.

"Where to?" Ryan asked, but he was pretty sure he knew the answer—the trestle. Bran surprised him by saying, "The Rock."

"Why The Rock?"

"It's closer. We can start there and make our way down-river."

* * *

There were two cars parked at The Rock when they got there. "Who do you think is here?" Bran asked.

"I don't know, but I'm going to hide my bow," Ryan said, and walked into the woods. When he returned, Bran was crouching at the base of The Rock, listening to the men who were throwing stones in the water.

Chapter 21

Summer, 1939

Chief Miller wasn't used to sitting in the passenger seat, but this was Larry Osborne's car so he couldn't very well ask to drive. The old galvanized boat tied to the top of the Chrysler must have weighed two hundred pounds, and the car's shocks had seen better days, so every bump in the dirt road through the woods shuddered up through the frame and into his ass.

When one particularly nasty bump threw Miller into the side door, Osborne looked over at him and said, "Not much further, Chief."

"Damn, Larry, why didn't we just put the boat in back at The Logs?"

"No could do, Chief," Osborne told him. "We'd never get past that shallow part at the rocks. The only place to put the boat in downstream of them is at the trestle."

"Fine," Miller mumbled, and then cursed under his breath as they hit the most vicious bump yet.

When they got to the trestle, Aaron Billings' car was gone.

Osborne backed into the open area in front of the trestle, got out of the Chrysler, and started untying the ropes that held the boat in place. When he had the last one off, he told Miller, "Give me a hand with this, will ya, Chief? She's a steady bitch, but she's heavy."

"How do you get this thing on and off when you're alone?" Miller asked as he struggled with his end of the boat.

"It ain't easy, I'll tell ya that," Osborne answered. "But if ya want to fish the river, the whole river, ya gotta do it."

"You ever think about a canoe, or a lighter boat?"

Osborne shook his head. "Fuck them canoes. Those things are for sissies and Indians. Me and Miss Jane here have been together for a long time, so I guess I'll be stickin' with her as long as I can."

Once they had the boat off and in the water, Osborne went back to the car for the motor, a two-horse Evinrude. Once it was in place at the stern, they were ready to search the river for young Billings.

"Upstream, or downstream?" Osborne asked as they backed away from the bank.

"Hell, he could have gone anywhere. Let's try upstream first."

"You got it," Osborne answered as he started the motor and turned the boat into the slow-moving current.

"Just take it slow," Miller told him, "I don't want to miss anything."

The river was only about twenty yards wide, and no more than five or six feet deep most of the way, so they were able to keep to the center. Miller kept watch on the left, and Osborne on the right. The water was crystal clear, and they could see all the way to the bottom. The river bed was covered by grasses that swayed in the current or patches of algae-covered gravel. Osborne had to navigate around an occasional tree that had fallen where the banks had been undercut by years of spring runoff. They made the half mile trip, and the only thing they saw were turtles that plopped into the water as they approached, some ducks, and a single great blue heron.

When they reached the rocks and could go no further, Miller said, "Okay, turn it around, but keep it slow and we'll switch sides just to make sure."

"You're the boss," Osborne answered, and swung the boat around to head downstream.

The trip back to the trestle proved no more fruitful than the trip up. They saw the same ducks, but the great blue was gone. This time, they chased a belted kingfisher downriver as they went. It would fly about fifty yards downstream, alight in a tree, and then take off again as they neared it.

"Okay, be sharp," Miller said as they passed under the trestle. Twenty yards downstream the water deepened for about fifty yards and they couldn't see the bottom. "We'll come back with a hook if we don't find anything further down," the Chief told Osborne.

The trip down the river to the lake was as fruitless as the one upriver to the rocks.

They found the body just after the river opened up to form a long, shallow lake that ended at the dam two miles down in West Milton. "What's that over in those lily pads?" Osborne said, pointing to something in the water about twenty feet from the boat.

Miller stood up, shaded his eyes for a better look, and saw the thing Osborne was pointing to—it was indeed a body. "That's it," he announced, and Osborne maneuvered the boat over to it. Just before they reached it, the lily pads near the body moved and Miller saw something under the surface dart away from it. "Wait," he said, and stared into the water. When he didn't see anything, he motioned for Osborne to go ahead.

The body was floating face down, trapped among the lily pads. It was out of place among the broad green leaves and bright white and yellow blossoms. The shirt it wore was shredded. Open wounds that had been washed clean of blood ran across its back. When Miller grabbed it by the shoulder and rolled it over, they were greeted by Billings' terrified face. With his mouth open, and his lips drawn back from his teeth, it looked it as if he were screaming at them.

Larry Osborne puked over the side of the boat before he managed a weak, "Jesus H. Christ on a crutch, what the fuck happened to him?"

"Snapping turtles," Chief Miller told him as they attempted to haul the body into Osborne's galvanized steel fishing boat. Billings' his shirt had been torn open and was hanging from his body in ribbons. There were deep gashes along the length of his torso.

"Jesus! In one day?"

"Well, there are a lot of them in the lake, and some of them are pretty damn big," Miller replied.

"Yeah, *but in one day*? And those look like cuts, not bites." Osborne argued.

"He must have bumped into some old junk when he floated down here. People dump all sorts of shit in the river. Let's just get him into the boat," Miller said as he grabbed the corpse's hair and reached for its arms.

"Fuck," Osborne said, and puked again once the body was in the boat.

Osborne did his best not to look at the body as they motored back to the trestle. When they got there, he refused to help the Chief drag it out of the boat. Then he flat out told Miller, "Sorry, Chief, but he's not going in my car."

"I never expected him to, Larry. You drive back to town,

stop at the station, and tell Dave Longo to drive down here with a body bag. I'll stay with him."

"Sure thing, Chief, that sounds good to me. Just help me get the boat loaded and out of here before I go. I don't think I'll be coming back here for a while."

"I can do that," Miller agreed.

When the boat was loaded and Osborne was ready to leave, the Chief told him, "Larry, only talk to Dave, and don't go spreading this around town. I'll know it was you if I hear anything. I want to tell Bob about his boy before he hears it from some waggle tongue on the street."

"Sure thing," Osborne replied. Miller hoped Larry could keep it to himself long enough for him to talk to Bob Billings.

* * *

The Chief sat in the shade of the trestle abutment facing the river as he waited for the ambulance to arrive. Aaron Billings' corpse lay on the ground between him and the water. It didn't take long for him to get a bad feeling about his situation, sitting alone next to the river with a ravaged corpse. He wasn't inclined to the jitters, but then again he wasn't used to hunting creatures out of a nightmare. Just to be safe, he took his revolver out of its holster and put it in his lap.

Thirty-five minutes later, Miller was lulled into a false sense of security by the unchanging flow of the river and the sleep-inducing heat of the day. He was checking his watch, wondering where Longo was, when something, some feral feeling, snapped his attention back to the river. It took him a few seconds to realize what he was seeing. The creature was out of the water and clawing its way toward Billings' corpse. In another foot it would be there, and then it was just a short six feet to where he sat. It had a reptilian face with small pointed horns on either side of its head. Its ice-blue eyes bore into him, sending a shiver down his spine.

Maybe it doesn't see me. Maybe it's coming after Billings. They sat like that, unmoving, for a full minute. *Easy, easy,* Miller thought as he inched his hand toward the revolver sitting in his lap. He had just managed to reach it when two clawed hands grasped Billings' corpse for support, and the creature started to drag itself over the body. Fear grabbed at Miller's heart as his hand clutched his revolver.

* * *

The noise of the boat's motor drew the oniare from its hunt for an acceptable host. It followed the men and their boat upriver, waiting for a chance to grab one of them. Either one would make an excellent host, but it wouldn't attack if they were together. It had learned that these creatures retrieved their dead.

When the boat stopped and turned to head downriver, the oniare sank to the bottom and clung to the trunk of a fallen tree where it was all but invisible from the surface. When the boat passed, it released its hold on the tree and followed the men downriver. When it passed the place where it had captured the poisoned host, it made an angry clicking that could only be heard underwater.

It followed them downstream until the river broadened into a large shallow lake. *What were they doing?* It got the answer when the men found the body of the poisoned host and dragged it into the boat. It lifted its head above the surface to watch them, and this time, a low hiss of anger and frustration escaped from the oniare's clenched jaws. The poisoned one was useless, but the fetus was still inside it.

Once they had the discarded host in the boat, the men

headed back upriver at a much faster pace than they had come down it. The oniare followed, but it couldn't match their pace and the distance between them soon widened. It caught up with them when they stopped at the place it had taken the poisoned one.

The oniare watched from across the river, hidden by the shadows of a branch that hung just above the water. When one man left and the second stayed with the body of the poisoned one, it knew its time had come. Now, if the man would just come near the water.

It crossed to the man's side of the river, moving slowly underwater. An observer from the trestle might have seen it, but the reflection of the sun off the water from where the man sat had turned the surface into a mirror. When it reached the bank, the oniare slid slowly from the water, using its claws to pull itself through the mud. It could have used its tail for added propulsion, but it couldn't afford to make too much noise. That would alert the human.

Out of the water, the oniare could breathe through its skin as long as it remained wet. If it started to dry out, it would need to return to the river. Since the path to the man was through the shade, it would have enough time to reach him, kill him, and force his mouth open enough to allow the fetus to enter his body through his throat. Then it could return to the river to immerse itself before returning to drag the body back. Once it had it, it would take the body to the lake and hide it so the others of its kind would never find it.

When it reached the poisoned one, something startled the man leaning against the stones. The oniare could see it in the man's eyes, the look of recognition that he was in danger. It grasped the corpse in front of it, intending to use it as a launching point.

* * *

Miller looked into the eyes of the creature stalking him and froze. Their eyes locked, and neither moved for what seemed like an eternity. Then he realized that if he didn't move, he was probably a dead man. Adrenalin and fear drove him, but his hand was shaking when he pulled the trigger of his revolver.

The first shot slammed into Billings' body, making it jump as if it had been kicked. The oniare immediately released the corpse, twisted its body like a snake and, using its claws and tail, launched itself toward the river. Miller's second shot kicked up a splash of water inches from the creature's head. The thing was gone before he got off a third, but Miller kept pulling the trigger until the hammer struck the first spent casing. His first thought after he relaxed enough to think was, *How the hell am I going to explain the bullet in Billings?*

Chapter 22

Summer, 1956

Ryan came out of the woods after stashing the bow and hunting arrows under a pile of leaves and saw Bran crouched at the base of The Rock. Bran put a finger to his lips for silence, and then motioned for Ryan to join him. Crouching low and walking as quietly as he could, Ryan approached The Rock and managed to join his friend without giving them away. He was about to ask what was going on, but Bran shushed him with a finger to his lips. A second later he heard voices from just over The Rock's crest.

"The damn thing ruined my life. I lost my confidence, and I had nightmares for years. The only reason I stayed on the force is because the Chief thought he owed me for the things I— we, went through that summer."

"What the hell *did* happen?" the second voice asked.

"After we pulled Sean McCauley, he was the first victim, from the river, I was out of commission for a few days because of my leg, but that didn't last long. A few days later, a

116

kid, Aaron Billings … well, he was twenty, got drunk down by the trestle that the lumber company had started to build but never finished. They were going to log the mountain on the other side of the river, but that fell through. Anyway, Billings never came home, and his father reported him missing. Normally we would have given him a day or so to show up, but after what had happened to McCauley … well, Chuck Turcott and the Chief went right out looking for him."

"Did they find him?"

"Not at first. They found his car and signs that something had been dragged into the river. Chief Miller went back with Larry Osborne. Larry had a boat, and they searched the river for him. They found his body in Cooper Lake, hung up in some lily pads. It was full of deep cuts, and his face looked as if he had died screaming. The Chief told Larry it was the work of snapping turtles. It was a lame excuse, but Larry didn't want to know any different."

At this point, Ryan was looking a bit green, but Bran squeezed his forearm and once again motioned him to be quiet. It wasn't easy, but he pushed down his growing unease and did as his friend asked.

"Are you sure it wasn't snapping turtles? I hear the lake is full of them," the second voice asked.

"Oh yeah, we're sure. After they got the body in the boat and hauled it back to the trestle, Osborne came back to the station and told me what had happened and that the Chief wanted me to go down there with a body bag and get the body."

"They just left it there?"

"No, but they should have. The Chief stayed there to watch over it while Osborne came back to town. We had quite a few stray dogs, foxes, and a sky full of turkey vultures back then. Hell, we still have a sky full of turkey vultures today;

they nest on the cliffs. The Chief didn't want anything to ravage the body while they were gone, that's why he stayed. From the way he told me later, he sort of drifted off while he was waiting for me and almost got himself killed."

"What happened?"

"The oniare came out of the river and clawed its way right up the bank before he snapped out of his daydreaming and managed to take a few shots at it. He missed, and it made it back to the water, but it almost had him."

"Jesus."

This was too much for Ryan, and he let out a soft moan. Bran gave him an angry look and tried to shush him, but it was too late.

"Did you hear that?" the first voice asked.

"Who's down there?" the second voice demanded.

"Ryan Lowell and Brandon Liotti," Ryan answered.

"Come up here, boys," the first voice told them.

Before Bran stood up, he gave Ryan a nasty look and punched him in the arm.

"Ow," Ryan said, and stood up, too.

"I thought I told you boys to stay away from the river?" Dave Longo said when Bran and Ryan joined them at the top of The Rock.

"How much of our conversation did you boys hear?" Erickson asked.

"Nothing," Bran told them at the same time that Ryan blurted out, "Everything."

"I'm going to assume it was everything," Dave said. "And from what you heard, and from what happened to *you*," he added, pointing to Bran, "you should realize you need to stay away from the river and let us take care of this thing."

"Yes, sir," Ryan said, looking down at his feet.

"What about you, Liotti?" Dave asked.

"I guess so," Bran answered after a minute of awkward silence.

"Good, now go home and stay away from the river," Erickson told them.

"And stay away from the lake, too," Longo added, knowing Bran was the more reckless of the two and would look for a way around their order to stay away.

"Yes, sir," both boys answered in unison.

"Good, now get out of here," Longo told them.

Bran started to walk up the dirt road toward the development, but before he went two steps, Ryan hissed, "What about my bow and arrows?"

"We'll come back for them after they leave," Bran answered.

When they were out of view of The Rock, Bran cut into the woods and led the way to the top of an outcropping from where they could watch The Rock and the two cars parked there.

"You think they'll listen?" Erickson asked.

"I hope so," Longo answered, and threw another rock into the water.

* * *

The oniare was drawn to the sound of the rocks hitting the water. It had been lurking at The Back Beach waiting for a single human to come near the shore, but the beach had remained deserted. It seemed the humans never showed up until the sun was moving further up the sky. Then it heard the splashes, faint but distinct. Somewhere upstream, something was throwing rocks in the water. Maybe it was the young one it had almost had the last time.

As it moved upstream, the barkless, slimy logs were hardly an impediment. All it took was one flick of its powerful tail and it easily slipped over them into the deeper water on the other side. It slowed and hugged the far bank as it got nearer to the source of the splashes. The sun was still low in the sky, and shadows from the overhanging small trees and bushes provided the perfect camouflage for its approach. When it slipped its head above water, it saw there were two humans on the top of The Rock, well out of reach, and it hissed in frustration. Nevertheless, it stayed in the shadows with just its eyes above the surface … waiting.

Splash … wait … *splash* … The humans sat on The Rock making noises the oniare found difficult to hear with its head above water. One of them, always the same one, would occasionally toss a stone into the river. The oniare would watch it arc through the air until it hit the water … *splash*. When it dipped its head below the surface where the sound carried much easier, the splash was like an explosion.

The oniare's interest peaked when the young one it had already tried to kill joined the older ones on The Rock. It had almost had this one twice and knew this one would eventually come back to the river, back to where it could kill it and plant the fetus within it. But then the young ones left and only the older ones remained.

Splash … Another stone hit the water.

* * *

"What now?" Erickson asked.

Longo looked at the river. His hands shook and his voice cracked as he fought some inner demon. "This is the closest I've been to the river since '39. I promised myself I'd never come back here, and here I am, hunting for the thing that's haunted my nightmares since the first day I saw it."

Erickson stared at him and then just shook his head.

"You going to be able to do this, Dave?"

"Oh yeah," Dave answered, "and this time I'm going to make sure that thing never comes back."

Chapter 23

June, 2014

Ryan knew it was time to take a ride. Time to drive the three hundred plus miles Google Maps told him it would take to get from his house in Mettabasset, Connecticut to Poquonock, Vermont. He just couldn't bring himself to get in the car and start driving. The suitcase he had packed for the trip had sat near the front door untouched for two weeks. *I'll leave tomorrow*, he kept telling himself, but tomorrow came and the suitcase never made it the twenty feet from the front door to the car's trunk.

Coward, he told himself as he looked at the suitcase on his way out the door. Then, on impulse, he grabbed it and practically ran to his car before he could lose his nerve. If he could just get in the car and get on the road, he knew he could make it, so he ripped open the driver's side door, tossed the suitcase into the passenger's side, got in, and put the key in the ignition. He almost snapped it in two turning it to start the engine. His hands didn't stop shaking until he was out of Mettabasset and on I-91 heading north.

After he passed through Springfield, Massachusetts, Ryan felt the pangs of hunger nibbling at his stomach. He was trying to decide where to stop and eat when he saw a sign for a Cracker Barrel restaurant in Holyoke. That sounded much more appealing than McDonalds or Burger King, so he kept driving.

When he pulled into the Cracker Barrel's parking lot, he already knew exactly what to expect. It had a log cabin feel, with rocking chairs sitting outside on a covered porch. Inside, he had to thread his way through shelves of merchandise that were just one step up from a Christmas Tree Shop.

He was thinking of just having a slice of apple pie and a cup of coffee, but before he could order, the waitress placed a plate full of eggs, bacon, and home fries in front of the customer at the next table. It looked and smelled so good that Ryan immediately changed his mind.

"You need a menu, hun, or do you know what you want?" the waitress asked when she got to him.

"No, I know what I want," Ryan answered. "I'll have two eggs over easy, home fries with onions, a side of sausage, and wheat toast."

"You want coffee with that?" she asked as she scribbled his order on her pad.

"Please," he responded. "Do you have half and half?"

She gave him an "are you kidding" look before answering, "No, but we have cream, milk, skim milk, or creamer."

"Cream," he answered.

Ryan watched her as she walked away. She was a caricature of every waitress he could remember from his youth—short, a little overweight, with dyed blond hair and a haggard look from too many hours spent walking back and forth between the kitchen and counter. She would put up with all the transients and their bullshit and smile while she did it.

For as crowded as the Cracker Barrel was, his breakfast came surprisingly quickly. "Here you go, hun," the waitress said as she placed his order in front of him. "Pay at the register on your way out," she said when she gave him his check, and then she was gone, on her way to pick up someone else's order.

When he was back on I-91, Ryan's mind drifted back to Poquonock and some of the good times he had shared with Bran. In some ways, even though Bran's dad was dead, Ryan had envied him because of it. His dad had been a long-haul trucker; Ryan only saw him on weekends, and even then they didn't do much together. At least Bran had his own bedroom and Ryan envied him that. He had had to share his with his sister. Man, had that been a pain. How many hours had they spent in Bran's room, small as it was, making model cars or reading comic books? It must have been hundreds.

Bran's room had been cool, like the ones on *Leave it to Beaver* or *Lassie.* Model airplanes hung from the ceiling on invisible fishing line, Yankees and Dodger pennants hung on the walls, and model cars sat on the dresser. Bran's bed was against one wall, and it was the *only* bed in the room. There were two beds in the room he and his sister shared. There was barely enough room for the one dresser. He got the top two drawers, his sister got the bottom two. Bran could keep his fishing pole in the corner of his room. Ryan had to keep his in the unfinished attic. Bran also had a drawer for his collections of baseball cards, stamps, bottle caps, and matchbook covers. Ryan's were kept in a box in the bedroom closet.

Thinking of those collections reminded Ryan of the horsehead bottle cap they had found the day after they had first seen the oniare. They had ridden their bikes into town and gone straight to the Pick & Pay Market to look for one that matched. They'd searched the racks but couldn't find it. Bran finally admitted they would have to go to Larry's Liquor Store to see if he knew what it was.

Ryan chuckled to himself when he remembered how nervous they had been standing in front of Larry's, trying to build up enough courage to go in. When they finally did, they were immediately accosted by Larry himself. Larry was, as his father would have said, "a crusty old bird."

"What do you boys want? There's nothing in here for you," he had thundered. Ryan remembered that he had been ready to turn around and walk right back out, but Bran, being Bran, had stood his ground and held out the bottle cap.

"We found this at The Back Beach and want to know if you know what it is," he said, holding out the cap.

"Well, let's see it," Larry said, holding out his hand.

Ryan handed it to him, and both boys stood in silence as Larry made a great show of examining it. Finally, he nodded his head and pointed to a cooler in the back. "It's from a bottle of Rolling Rock. I don't get much call for it, it being a *premium* beer and all that, but I keep a six-pack or two on hand for Glenn Haskens. He don't drink Schlitz or Ballantine like most folks in this town. Here, let me show you," he offered, and took them to the rear of the store.

Ryan laughed at his own naiveté as he remembered being awed by the bottles of scotch, whiskey, and wine that filled the shelves and lined the walls. The store was no more than twenty feet deep, but it seemed endless to him back then.

Larry opened the cooler, reached in, and grabbed a six-pack. "See, here it is," Larry said, showing it to the boys. Sure enough, each bottle was topped with the mirror image of the cap Bran held in his hand.

"Cool," Ryan said, and held out his hand to retrieve the oddity, knowing Bran would be dying to get one of his own.

"Let's go look for another one," Ryan had suggested as they left Larry's.

"Nah, let's see if anybody's at the school playing basketball," Bran had answered.

Ryan was drawn out of his reverie when the voice on his GPS demanded he take the next exit. He did, and it dropped him on Main Street in Poquonock. It was strangely familiar yet disturbingly different at the same time.

Chapter 24

Summer, 1939

Screw this, Miller thought as he reloaded his revolver. *There's no way I'm staying anywhere near the water.* He started to back away from the river, but knew he couldn't just leave Billings' body on the bank where that thing might come back for it.

What the hell am I going to do?

It took him a minute to realize that he had been leaning back against the answer to his problem for the last thirty-five minutes. The top of the trestle was where he needed to be. He had never been much of a climber, but, two broken nails and couple of raw fingers later, he conquered the climb and was looking down at Billings' corpse and the river. The creature was nowhere in sight.

Normally he might have admired the view from his perch, but today it just added to his growing feeling of desperation. The sun made the water's surface sparkle when it rippled in the wind. In those places, it looked like a mirror whose face was dancing in the wind. When the breeze wasn't whipping the surface, the blue sky and incredibly white clouds were reflected back at him. The only places he could actually see into the water to the bottom was where the shadow of the trestle, or overhanging greenery along the bank, eliminated the mirroring effect. The damned thing could be right below him and he'd never be able to see it. Knowing that, he sat with his revolver in his lap so he could get off a quick shot at the thing just in case it appeared.

Miller heard the car coming before he could see it, so he lowered his body over the edge of the abutment until he was hanging by his fingertips. *God, what if it comes out while I'm hanging here?* he thought, and quickly let go and dropped to the ground. He was scrambling to his feet and nervously checking out the river when the car came around the bend and into sight. When it did, he saw it was Tom Blakely's hearse.

Blakely pulled up, and Miller was surprised to see Dave Longo get out of the passenger side. "Dave, what the hell are you doing here? I thought I told you to stay back at the station."

"Yeah, well, Tom had no idea how to get back here, so someone had to show him the way. I could have sent Pete Costentino, but ... you know."

Miller did know. He had inherited Pete from the former Chief. Pete was a volunteer. He could help out when they needed an extra body to direct traffic on the 4th of July, or answer phones if one of them was out sick, but for anything that required the least bit of discretion, Pete was not the guy you wanted. If Pete knew something, the whole town would know about it within hours.

"So who's in the office?" Miller asked.

Longo shrugged and then answered, "Pete—I couldn't get anyone else."

While they were talking, Tom got out and went around back to open the tailgate to get the stretcher. "Where's the body?" he asked.

"Over there on the bank. You and I can get him while Dave keeps an eye on the river in case the thing that did this comes back."

"What *thing* are you talking about and what do you mean *comes back?*" Blakely wanted to know.

"I'll tell you when we get back to your place. Right now I just want to get him out of here."

"Jesus Christ," Longo said, recoiling in surprise when he saw the body. Blakely didn't say anything, but Miller could see that the wheels were turning in Tom's head. I'm *going to have to tell him the whole story once we get back to his funeral parlor.*

"Keep that gun handy," Miller told Longo, nodding at the revolver on Dave's hip. Then he turned to Blakely and said, "Let's go, I don't want to waste any time doing this. We go down, get him on the stretcher, and get out."

Longo watched from the top of the bank as the chief and Blakely made their way to the body, quickly lifted it onto the stretcher, and got back up the bank without any problems. After that, it only took a few minutes to get the body into the back of the hearse. Then the three of them crammed into the hearse's front seat and drove back to Tom's funeral home.

"So what's going on here?" Blakely demanded after they had transferred Billings' body to the table in his basement.

Longo looked at the Chief, waiting for him to speak. Miller was silent for a minute before telling Blakely what he wanted to know. "There's a creature in the river. Chuck Turcott calls it an oniare, along with another name we can't pronounce. He says it's part of an old race that was here before the Indians, even. Turcott says it shows up in the river every once in a while. When it does, it kills and eats people. His father fought and killed one the last time it happened. It has to be the thing that killed that drifter, Sean McCauley, and young Billings. I saw it today, and it's right out of a nightmare or some weird horror story."

"Tell me all about this creature," Blakely demanded.

Miller fidgeted a bit, as if unwilling to say what had happened, but once he started, he told the entire story of his encounter with the creature.

"Damn," Longo said. It was almost a whisper, and Miller nearly missed it.

"Damn is right," the Chief agreed.

"What did the thing look like? You said it could have been something out of aa horror story," Blakely asked.

The Chief shook his head as if he was loath to even think about the creature. "It was like a big snake, at least ten feet long, and thick. Its face was definitely reptilian, but it had ice-blue eyes, not just the iris, but the entire eye, and I could see intelligence in them. It had two small horns, one on either side of its face. But the thing that really scared me was the arms. It had two long, skinny arms and huge hands. The fingers were tipped by long, wicked-looking, yellow claws."

When he heard that, Longo unconsciously touched his injured leg.

"This makes two people this thing has killed—that we know of. What are you going to do about it?" Blakely wanted to know.

"What I don't want to do is create a panic or a circus around here. If word gets out that there's a monster in the river, every cowboy with a gun within a hundred miles will show up wanting to be the one who bagged the damn thing. If that happens, someone's going to get shot for sure. And if they don't find it, we're going to look like damned fools."

"I have to admit, that makes sense," Blakely agreed.

"So, any ideas?" Miller asked.

"Let's take a look at the body, and I'll see what I can do," Blakely answered. "You coming?" he said to the chief as he led the way from the room to his workspace.

"No, I've seen as much as I want to see. You can go if you want, Dave, but I'll stay right here."

"Yeah, I'll go. I guess one of us should," Longo answered.

Longo really hadn't gotten much of a look at the body back at the trestle. Now he could see just how much damage the creature had inflicted on it. An actual chill ran up his spine, and he shuddered thinking about what Billings must have gone through. His mouth was open as if he had died screaming. His torso was covered in long, deep gashes like the ones in Dave's own leg. Looking at the body, Longo knew just how lucky he had been to escape the oniare when it had grabbed him.

Blakely was talking to himself as he performed his examination of the body. "I can close the jaw, no problem there, and, except for that, his face is untouched … that's good. I can stitch all the wounds and then I can cover it all with his funeral suit. If I do all that, he can have an open-casket funeral and none of this will be visible. Yes, that works," he finally said, then added, "Let's go tell the Chief."

Longo took one more look at young Billings, thinking, *Jesus, that could have been me,* when he saw a bulge appear in the corpse's stomach. "Tom, wait. What the hell is that?"

Blakely was about to answer when a one-inch long claw broke through Billings' stomach. Blakely recoiled like he had been slapped, Longo was reaching for his revolver when a second, and then a third, claw broke through. A fourth started to emerge when they all shivered once and then drew back into the body.

"Jesus Christ," Blakely swore, "what the hell was that?"

"A little one of those things," Longo said, aiming his pistol at the corpse.

"You mean there's one inside it, and it's alive?" Blakely asked. Longo could hear panic and disgust in his voice.

Longo felt a hot flash of hate and anger wash over his entire body. He wanted nothing more than to empty his revolver into Billings' corpse where the claws had appeared, but he stopped himself just before pulling the trigger. Instead, he took a six-inch folding knife from his pocket and flipped it open. "Not for long," he told Blakey as he approached the corpse.

"Wait. Let me use this," Blakely said, holding up a scalpel. His voice was shaking. "Just make sure you kill it when I open him up."

"Right," Longo agreed, and placed the barrel of his revolver an inch from Billings' stomach as Blakely prepared to slice it open. "Go ahead," he said when he was ready.

Blakey stood alongside Longo, reached in front of him, and inserted the scalpel just below Billings' breastbone. Then, in one continuous motion, he sliced the body open to the groin before jumping back, away from Longo and the corpse.

Longo was ready to shoot anything that moved, but nothing did. He used his knife to pry open the wound that Blakely had made, and then gagged at the foul smell that emerged from the corpse. It smelled like rotting meat and alcohol. "Jesus," he swore as he fought the urge to vomit.

Blakely, who was used to the odor of death, still looked shocked at the smell that emanated from Billings. "God, that's awful. What the hell is it? Is that thing alive?" he asked as he inched closer.

Longo used the flat of his knife to open the wound and look

inside the corpse. There was a foot-long, miniature version of the oniare inside Billings—that and little else. The thing had consumed most of his internal organs. "I don't think so," Longo said, and poked at it with his knife. When the creature didn't move, he used the blade to lift it from the body and placed it on Billings' chest.

"What do you think killed it?" Longo asked as he poked at the shriveled body of the little oniare.

Blakely came closer, looked at the creature's skin, and got a stronger whiff of the smell coming from it. When he leaned even closer to get a better look at it, the creature's ice-blue eyes fluttered open and it hissed at him.

Longo stepped in when Blakely staggered back from the table. "Time to die, you little fucker," he spat at the creature. When he stuck the blade of his knife into its open mouth, its hiss turned into a muffled gurgle. It was still twitching when Longo pulled it from Billings' corpse and repeatedly struck at it with the knife until pieces of it were scattered over Billings, the table, and the floor.

When Long's fury was finally final spent, Blakely stepped back to the table and looked inside Billings' empty body cavity. When he saw what was there, he succumbed to the urge to vomit.

"Alcohol poisoning," he told Longo as he wiped the puke off his chin. "You can smell it, and it looks like it's been pickled. Billings must have been drunk as a skunk, and the thing poisoned itself eating his organs."

Then Blakely stepped back, stared at Billings and asked, "But how did it get inside his body?"

The cop in Longo had already solved that mystery. "Through his mouth and down his throat. That's why his mouth is frozen open like that."

"Christ," Blakely muttered, and threw up again. When

he looked back up at Longo, he saw that Dave was laughing. "What's so funny Dave?" he demanded, thinking Longo was mocking him.

"I was just thinking. If there was one of these in Mc-Cauley—we buried that little fucker alive. How's that for payback?"

Chapter 25

Summer, 1956

Longo pitched his last stone into the river and peered into the water to see if the oniare had answered his call. When he didn't see anything, he stood up, brushed off the seat of his pants, and turned to Erickson. "Let's walk the path. We can leave the cars here and come back for them later."

"What path?" Erickson asked.

"The one that runs along the bank on this side. It goes from here to the rocks. After that, it's spotty from the rocks to the trestle. Or at least it was back in my day."

"Well, then, lead the way," Erickson told him.

As Dave climbed down The Rock, the world seemed to take on a sharper focus. He noticed that sometime between '39 and now, someone had poured a concrete platform for a diving board. Rusted bolts stuck up out of the cement, but the board, if there had ever been one, was long gone. As he neared the river, the smell of it washed over him. It was clean and sharp, with a hint of moisture on the breeze that rippled its surface. The sky seemed to become a deeper blue and the clouds a brighter white. Every sense he had was on full alert.

Erickson followed Longo down The Rock and onto the well-worn path that ran along the river. This, he realized, was how the boys had managed to get to The Logs the day that kid had been killed. The path was hard packed dirt that dipped and climbed with the land. Exposed roots crossed it like the veins on the back of an old man's hands. After he stumbled on the first one, his attention was split between the river and the path. Dave, on the other hand, never took his eyes off the water. He moved with an unexpected grace that amazed Erickson. Once, the path dipped right down to the river's edge, and as Longo approached it, a large bullfrog croaked and leapt off the bank and into the river. Erickson, city boy that he was, thought it was the creature and almost shot his own foot trying to get his revolver out of its holster.

"Jesus, Marty, it's just a frog. Calm down," Dave told him when he turned and saw Erickson trying to get his gun out of its holster.

"Right," Marty answered, chastised and embarrassed. As they began walking again, blue jays in the branches over-head started screaming at them. "Fucking boondocks," he mumbled under his breath.

When they reached The Logs, visions of the dead kid's face jumped into Marty's head. *Jesus, I never want to see anything like that again.*

"Marty, you okay?" he heard Longo say. Thoughts of the past disappeared to be replaced by Dave Longo shaking his arm and staring into his eyes.

"Yeah, I'm fine. What's next?"

"The Back Beach," Longo told him and picked up the path where it started just past the parking area at The Logs.

Longo hadn't seen the beach yet—it hadn't been there in '39—but he had passed it on his drive to The Rock. It was right behind the ball field that hadn't been there then, either.

"Why do they call it 'The Back Beach'? That doesn't make any sense to me?" Marty asked as he followed Dave onto the path.

"I have no idea. It's just always been The Back Beach. Just like 'The Rock' has always been The Rock and 'The Logs' have always been The Logs. Who knows where names like that come from?" Dave answered. "You must have had things like that where you grew up, didn't you?"

"Yeah, I guess we do," Marty answered, thinking about "The Bridge." There were dozens of bridges in the city, but if you said "The Bridge," everyone knew exactly which one you were talking about. The others were the Jefferson Street Bridge or the Bank Street Bridge, but "The Bridge" was just The Bridge. He was still thinking about that when he almost ran into Longo's back. Dave was standing as still as a statue, shading his eyes, and staring intently at the water.

* * *

Ryan and Bran watched from their perch on the ridge as Dave Longo drew one last stone from his bag and tossed it toward the river. It arced up and then fell out of sight. They couldn't see it hit the water or hear the splash from where they were. After a minute, Longo stood up, wiped the seat of his pants with his hands, and said something to Erickson. When Erickson stood up, both men climbed down The Rock, and moved out of sight as they headed toward the river. They appeared a minute later on the path to The Logs. They were only visible for a few seconds before the trees hid them.

Bran jumped up and said, "Let's go!"

"Where?" Ryan wanted to know.

"To get your bow, you idiot. You can't leave it there—someone might find it."

"Oh yeah, but then we're going home so I can put it away," Ryan told him. And before Bran could argue, he said, "We can come back tomorrow when Mister Longo and the other cop are gone. If they see us with the bow, they'll know what we're doing."

He could tell Bran didn't like it from the way he said, "Fine, but we *are* coming back. We're going to kill that thing."

* * *

The oniare watched the men from the shadows. Just the top of its head and eyes were above water. It stood the risk of being seen, but knew it could dip under the water and disappear in an instant. When the men stood up and came toward the river, it slipped beneath the surface and sank to the bottom.

The oniare stayed motionless for a few minutes before rising to the surface to see what the men were doing. It was just in time to see them disappear on the path along the river. After a minute, it followed behind them, waiting for the chance to get one of them alone.

The men moved along the bank, appearing and disappearing in the trees and bushes that lined the river. There were very few places where the path actually came right down to the water's edge. It knew what they were doing; they were looking for it. It wondered what they would do if it showed itself to them. It knew that when it came to the shallow spot with the submerged logs, it might not have a choice if it wanted to follow them further.

The oniare waited and watched as the men approached the water at the shallow place. They stopped well away from the river and stared out toward the opposite bank. It was getting ready to slap the water to draw their attention when they turned and started walking downriver again. The first time they disappeared behind the trees along the bank the oniare used its claws and powerful tail to propel itself almost silently across the submerged logs. It could tell the men still had no idea it was stalking them. The oniare decided to act just before they reached the place that had been cleared of trees and bushes. It raised its head above the water and hissed at them. The fat one in the lead froze, but the taller, thinner one following him didn't seem to hear it.

Both men's eyes scanned the water, and when it was obvious they still hadn't seen it, the oniare lifted itself higher above the surface and hissed at them again. This time they did see it, and again, the fat one reacted first. It grabbed something in its hand and pointed it in its direction. Then there was a loud noise and the water exploded an inch from its head. It dove quickly and was gone before the next explosion disrupted the water above it.

* * *

Ryan was just picking up his bow when a gunshot broke the silence of the morning. "Leave it," Bran called. "I think they're shooting at it."

Ryan hesitated for a minute, not sure what to do, before stashing the bow and arrows back under the tree. When he got to the road, Bran was bouncing back and forth on his feet. "Let's go, let's go!" he demanded as Ryan stumbled from the woods. Then the two of them were running toward The Back Beach.

Ryan pulled up with a stitch in his side when they reached The Logs. Bran ran twenty yards further before stopping. Both boys stood in the road sucking wind and holding their sides. Ryan was the first to stand up straight. "Let's walk," he managed to say when he reached his friend. Bran was still breathing hard, so he just nodded in agreement.

Bran was the first to see Longo and Erickson standing on the bank halfway between The Logs and the beach. "There they are. Let's go see if they got it."

"No," Ryan answered. "They told us to go home. Let's hide and watch what happens. If they got it, we can come out. If they didn't, they won't know we didn't go home. I don't want them to go to my house and talk to my mom. She'd ground me for sure."

"Good idea," Bran agreed, and they faded into the woods.

Chapter 26

Summer, 1939

The entire town knew that Aaron Billings had been found in Cooper Lake and they knew about the condition of his body. Tom was actually amazed that Larry Osborne had been able to keep the story to himself for as long as he had. It had given Miller the time he needed to break the news to Bob Billings and for Tom Blakely to do what he could to clean up the body. His major concern had been to close young Aaron's jaw before his father saw him. Thankfully, he had managed to do that. There was nothing he could do to close the massive hole in Billings' torso or replace the internal organs, but he could cover those with a clean, white sheet. He was just doing that when the front doorbell rang. *That must be Bob,* he thought, and gave his work one last inspection before he went to meet the man.

The doorbell rang again before he reached it. "Coming," he called, in what he hoped was a calming voice. When he got to the door and opened it, he was surprised to find Chuck

Turcott.

"Chuck, can I help you?" he asked.

"I need to see Billings' body," Turcott told him.

If Blakely had been surprised to see Turcott at his door, he was shocked at the request. "I'm sorry, Chuck, but that's impossible. His family hasn't even seen him yet."

"Did you have to break his jaw to close his mouth? Did you stitch up all the cuts? Osborne's saying snapping turtles got him, but we both know that's a lie, don't we, Tom? Did Miller tell you about the creature that did this? Did he tell you about the oniare?"

Blakely stepped back at the mention of the creature. "He said he saw something out of a horror story."

"He saw it? Damn," Turcott said, and turned on his heel, leaving Blakely to stare at his back and wonder what was going on now.

* * *

Turcott stormed into the police station and found the Chief and Longo sitting in the Chief's office. "You saw it! You saw the oniare and you never bothered to tell me? Worse, you went looking for it without me. That was foolish. Did you hear nothing that I told you? That thing is dangerous. Did you tell Osborne what he was dealing with, or did you let him go out there blind?"

He saw a flash of anger in Miller's eyes, but it quickly died, and the man looked away.

"Hold on there ..." Longo started to say, coming to the Chief's defense, but Miller cut him off.

"No, Dave, he's right. I didn't appreciate it before, but I do now. Sit down, Chuck, and I'll tell you the whole story."

Turcott listened, never saying a word until Miller got to

the point where he realized the creature was crawling across the river bank, stalking him.

"You saw it? What did it look like, exactly?" Turcott demanded.

Miller took a minute to gather his thoughts before speaking. "The first thing I saw was the face. It looked like a snake … No, that's wrong. It looked reptilian, but not exactly like a snake. It was all sharp angles and …" He closed his eyes to picture it better. "… small, pointed scales. Its eyes were ice blue, like pictures I've seen of icebergs. It had small horns on either side of its head, no more than bumps really, but they were pointed. When it opened its mouth to hiss at me, it had sharp, pointed teeth on top and bottom."

Miller shook his head at this point. After a pause to collect himself, he went on. "I didn't see the hands until it reached up and put them on Billings' body. It sunk these long claws into Billings and it looked like it was going to use his corpse to pull itself along. That's when I grabbed my gun and shot at it. I'm kicking myself for not taking the time to aim. I hit Billings instead of the creature." Here he paused again. Both Longo and Turcott were leaning forward in their chairs waiting for him to go on.

"After that first shot, the damned thing moved like lightning. It used its arms to push back off Billings and twisted its body damn near in half to head back to the river. I'd say it was about ten feet long with a snake's body. It didn't taper to a point like the snakes I've seen; instead, it stayed as wide as the body all the way down. It did flatten out like a big flipper, though, so it must be fast as hell in the water."

"You said it had hands," Turcott said when it looked like Miller was done talking. "Did they grow right out of its body like fins, or did it have arms?"

"Arms. Long, skinny arms with one joint, just like an

elbow," Miller said, and then he was through talking.

"Amazing," Turcott finally said. "You must be the only person who's seen it up close and personal and lived to tell the story."

"I don't think I would be if it had gotten to me. I have no doubt the thing would have killed me," Miller said with conviction.

"So what do we do now?" Longo asked.

"You don't do anything. With that leg, you'd be more of a handicap than a help."

Dave started to argue, but Miller held up a hand to stop him, and Turcott said, "The Chief's right. That thing is fast, and if we have to move quickly, you might not be able to. You could wind up getting yourself, or one of us, killed."

Miller looked at Turcott and realized the decision had already been made—he was going to be a part of this. There was no doubt he was up to it, even if he was fifty-three. He was short, no more than five-feet-five, but there wasn't an ounce of fat on the man from what Miller could see. He wore his black hair long, Indian-style, in a braid, and the first streaks of grey were just starting to weave their way through it. His hands were calloused from years of working outdoors, and everyone in town knew he spent more time in the woods hunting, fishing, and trapping than he spent out of them. If they were going to kill this thing, Turcott was probably going to be the one who did it.

"So, what do you expect me to do, just sit here and mind the store while you two are out trying to kill this thing?" Longo asked.

"Exactly. Well … that and everything else that needs to be done around here to keep Poquonock running smoothly," Miller told him.

Dave didn't like it, but Miller *was* the Chief.

* * *

"The oniare is a predator, but so are we," Turcott told Miller. "You must remember that. If you relax your guard, or let your mind drift, it will kill you. It's much better at this than we are, so we must always stay together. I don't think it will attack us if we're together. I don't know that for sure, but I think so."

"What about that iron thing you told us about?" Miller wanted to know. "Is it true? Is iron the only thing that can kill it?"

"I don't think so. I just think it was the best thing my people had. You saw it. It's a flesh-and-blood creature. To us, it was a legend, a God, and the only way to kill a god is with the best weapons you have. I think lead will do just fine."

His people, the Iroquois, Miller thought. *Funny, I never knew Turcott was Iroquois. I never realized there were any of them left around here.*

* * *

"Try not to make noise … and don't disturb the water," Chuck told Miller as they sat in Turcott's kitchen sipping hot coffee. "Don't even talk once we're near the river. Keep your gun out and ready when I'm setting the traps, and try not to hit me if you can help it. If the oniare does manage to grab me, I'll do my best to keep it from dragging me into the water. If that happens, don't worry about hitting me. Shoot us both if you have to."

"What? I couldn't do that!"

"You better. I'll sure as hell need you to. You *might* kill me if you shoot me; the oniare will *definitely* kill me if you don't."

"How many of those things have you got?" Miller asked, nodding at the bundle of traps Turcott had brought up from his basement.

"A lot, but I'm only bringing six. They'll only work once, and I don't want to catch a muskrat or a raccoon. This thing is smart, and I don't want to let it know what they're for."

"How are you going to set them?"

"Not like I normally would. Normally, I'd put a stake in the ground underwater so once the muskrat trips it, the trap will hold it underwater and drown it. That won't work with the oniare. We want to keep it out of the river if we can," Turcott said.

"How are you going to do that?"

"With this," Turcott told him, and held up a spool of steel wire. "I'm going to tie one end around a tree about twenty yards from the water and attach the other end to the trap. If it springs the trap, we can shoot it where it is, or drag it up the bank and kill it there. Hopefully, we won't have to get anywhere near it."

"That should work," Miller said, fingering the revolver at his hip. *At least I sure as hell hope it will.*

Chapter 27

June, 2014

The drive down Main Street was part nostalgia, part discovery. The Casa Loma, the largest restaurant in town, had been replaced by a Shell station and a 7-Eleven. There was now a shopping plaza with a Stop & Shop and several smaller stores across the street. Ryan couldn't remember what had been there, but it certainly hadn't been a shopping plaza. The nearest thing they had had to a grocery store back then was the Pick & Pay, and it only took up the first floor of one of the old buildings downtown. The entire thing would have fit in the produce section of the new supermarket. He had to admit this was progress; people wouldn't have to drive another five miles to Lebanon to buy their groceries, but it dealt a savage blow to his memories.

Guy's Diner was gone, of course. It had closed up the year before he left. Now he couldn't even remember where it had been exactly. But Bill Paterson's house was still there, and he smiled at the memory of eating every ripe strawberry in Mrs. Paterson's garden when she told him he could help himself. He had never been invited back there again.

Hello, what's this? Ryan thought when he discovered a Dairy Queen just before reaching downtown. *Bran would have loved this.* He had planned on having a decent lunch, but there was a Heath Bar Blizzard in there calling his name—*dessert can wait until dinner,* he thought as he made a quick right into the parking lot.

As he sat in his car enjoying the Blizzard, he contemplated what he would do next. If he turned right after he left the DQ, he would be entering the old development that contained the first hundred or so four-room, eight-hundred square foot homes built after WWII for the soldiers returning home with a few thousand dollars of mustering-out pay in their pockets. From there the road would lead to the new development, where several hundred more of the cracker boxes had been built a few years later. If he stayed on Main Street, he would pass through downtown, and eventually reach the road the high school was on.

He wasn't sure which way he wanted to go, so he dug a quarter out of his pocket. *You decide,* he thought as he flipped the coin into the air: heads, he would head into the developments; tails, he would drive down Main Street. He caught it in his palm and flipped it over onto his wrist. When he took his hand away and looked, George Washington was looking back. *Fuck that,* he thought, and started on his drive down Main Street. The developments would take him too close to the road to The Back Beach.

For the first block, things were pretty much unchanged … the hardware store was now a beauty shop and nail salon. The other stores that had been there had faded from his memory long ago, but the buildings were still there—a little more worn to be sure, but it was still the Poquonock of his childhood.

The next block, however, was a cacophony of images, the new mixing with the old in a mishmash that made no sense to him at all. On the left, the entire block was now a shopping center with buildings that were three stories tall. The ground floor was lined with storefronts, but half were empty. From the signs on the front, the second floor was filled with offices. He had no idea what was on the third floor. It was all bright and shiny, like a new penny, and its newness only emphasized the age of the buildings on the other side. He supposed if he had been there when the new buildings went up, they wouldn't seem so out of place, but he was seeing them for the first time, and they screamed at him in their newness. He didn't think he could ever get used to them, not that he would have to. He didn't intend on staying all that long.

Chapter 28

Summer, 1939

"Might as well have another cup of coffee while I work on these," Turcott told the chief as he prepared the first trap on the floor between his knees. "I want to get as much of this done as possible before we get to the river."

Miller sat and watched as Turcott threaded the end of the steel wire through the handle of the next leg trap. Then he used a metal clip to clamp it off before unwinding about twenty yards of wire off the spool. As he unwound it, he re-wound it around his hand. When he had as much wire as he needed, he snipped it with wire cutters and tied off the loop he had made with a piece of twine. The whole operation only took a few minutes. Then he started on the next one.

"I've been thinking," he told Miller as he worked, "that you shouldn't be too close to me as I set the traps. If the oniare is there, it might not come out if it sees two of us. How good a shot are you with a rifle?"

"Pretty good," Miller answered. "At least I was. I haven't

shot one in a while."

"Just pretty good? That's not exactly what I wanted to hear," Turcott told him. "Maybe I should let you set the traps, and I'll stand back a ways with the rifle."

"We could do that," Miller answered, but he didn't sound all that sure of himself. "You'll have to teach me how to set the traps, though."

Miller watched as Turcott went through the steps of setting a trap. Then he tried it. He placed the trap on the floor and held it in place as he stepped down on the handle. As the two parts of the handle compressed, the jaws of the trap opened until they lay flat on the floor. Now came the tricky part, he had to set it. This consisted of latching the trip mechanism to the pan. It took a steady hand … and Miller didn't have one. After several tries, and almost losing a finger, it was apparent that idea was not going to work.

"How's Dave with a rifle?" Turcott finally asked.

"Well, he spent four years in the Army. We could ask him," Miller answered.

* * *

"What kind of rifle?" Dave wanted to know when Miller asked him. When Chuck Turcott heard this, he started to feel a whole lot better.

"Thirty-ought-six, open sights," he said as he handed the rifle to Longo.

Dave took the weapon, checked to make sure it was unloaded even though the bolt was already open, and Turcott knew he wanted Dave holding it when he set the traps.

The Chief wasn't crazy about turning the job over to Dave. He even suggested they all go together, but Turcott argued against it. Two people could *almost* be quiet in the woods. With three, it would be impossible. He didn't want to draw the oniare's attention until he was ready. Once the traps were set, he intended to make just enough noise to draw it in.

"I'll drive," Turcott said as they left the station. "We can take my car. It's less conspicuous than yours."

Longo had to agree to that; a black-and-white police car would make quite a stir after what had happened to Billings if anyone saw it heading into the woods.

Turcott retraced the route Chief Miller had taken two days before in search of the Billings boy. He pulled to the side and parked just before the corner that led to the trestle. "We walk from here," he told Longo. Dave nodded in agreement, and neither of them spoke again.

When Dave had the rifle, now loaded with a shell in the chamber, and Turcott had his string of traps, they started off toward the trestle. Dave was limping, but not badly. They went slowly so as not to make too much noise. Dave was amazed at how silent Turcott was, even carrying six large steel traps.

When they got to a place where they had a good view of the river and the trestle, Turcott put a hand on Longo's arm and motioned for him to stay there. Dave did, and Turcott continued on by himself. When he was within twenty yards of the water, he started to look for a tree to anchor the traps to. He found one without much trouble. It was a white oak with a trunk that was four inches in diameter. *This will do,* he thought, and carefully tied off the ends of wires and laid the traps out on the ground.

Dave took up his position with the rifle as Turcott carefully carried the first trap to the water. He had to constantly fight with the coiled wire to make sure it didn't kink or turn itself into a knot. When he reached the river's edge, he care-fully locked the trap's jaws open, set it on the bank of the river bed, sprinkled a little sand on the pan, and backed away to look at his handiwork. *That won't do*, he thought, and went into the woods for a stake. When he found one that would serve his purpose, he returned and staked the trap to the bank. Then he came back for another trap and another stake.

Turcott was setting the third trap when a feeling of unease stood the hairs on his arm on edge. Some sixth sense warned him he was in danger, and he leapt back from the river's edge. He was starting to feel a bit foolish until the water erupted into a shower of foam, teeth, and claws. The oniare would have had him if one of the traps he had already set hadn't clamped tight on the claws of its right hand.

"Chuck, jump aside!" he heard Longo yelling, and realized he was in Dave's line of fire. The oniare was still trying to get at him. Its other clawed hand was mere inches from his face. The sight of the creature's gaping mouth was the last thing he saw before he flung himself backward. When he hit the ground, he rolled to the right, out of Dave's line of fire.

Turcott heard the crack of the shot and saw the oniare jerk back as if hit by an invisible blow. He heard a high-pitched, hissing scream from the wounded creature and Longo working the bolt to jack another bullet into the rifle's barrel, then there was a splash and the oniare was … gone.

"Where did it go?" Longo shouted as he rushed to the bank, searching the water for the creature. His efforts were in vain; even the ripples from where it had gone back into the river were gone, swept away by the current. Turcott stood up and pointed to the trap that had just saved his life. The stake he had used to pin it had held. In its jaws were two wicked-look-ing claws. They were slightly yellowed except at the base, where bits of dark, bloody flesh clung to them.

Turcott bent to retrieve the trap that had kept him out of the oniare's grasp. The monster had almost pulled the stake free. All it took was two quick tugs and it popped out of the ground. If Longo hadn't hit it with his first shot, the creature would have had him for sure. He was prying the jaws open to retrieve the claws when he realized Longo was standing next to him staring at the river.

"Jesus, Dave. That was close. If you hadn't hit it ..."

Longo didn't answer. He stood there for a long minute before he dropped to his knees and started shaking. The adrenaline rush was wearing off, and the enormity of what he had just witnessed hit him hard.

When Turcott saw what was happening, he jumped to Longo's side. If the oniare attacked again, Longo would be defenseless.

"Dave ... DAVE!" he shouted to get Longo's attention. "We need to get away from the water."

Longo didn't stop shaking, but he allowed Turcott to lead him away from the bank. When they were twenty feet from the river, Turcott let go of him and Longo sank to his knees and covered his face with his hands. Turcott placed his hand on Longo's shoulder to let him know he was there.

It was a full five minutes before Dave stood up and looked back at the river. Turcott saw his face turn from a look of shock to one of grim determination. "I'm going to kill that thing even if it means I have to die trying," Longo told him through gritted teeth.

* * *

The oniare had watched as the man placed something in the water. There was a second man, but he was too far away to be either a threat or prey. That was good—he only needed the one. When it had him, it would hide the host where the others would never find it.

It almost attacked when the man stood and walked away from the shore, but its hiding place was too far away, and it did not want to lose him by acting too soon. So it waited and watched, and when the man started to come back to the river's edge, it began to move across the river in a slow, cautious approach. It was getting ready to attack when the man jumped back. Something it had done must have alarmed him. Fearing the host of the fetus growing inside was escaping, it surged ahead, determined to grab the man and drag him into the river where it would force his mouth open and give the young one the gift it required.

It was almost there, it almost had him, and then something grabbed its claws and would not let go. It fought to reach the man, but then something else slammed into its body and threw it backward. Pain the oniare had never felt before ignited like a fire within it, and it launched itself back toward the river. The violence of its struggle with the thing that held it, and the force of its effort to reach the water, tore two of its claws from its hand, and more pain flooded its body. For the first time in its existence, the oniare retreated in fear, looking for the safety of deep water.

The oniare fled to the lake. The water there was deeper than the river, and it was wide and long. There were patches of water lilies and grasses, places to hide and heal. It had lost two claws on its injured hand, but that was minor compared to the wound it had suffered to its body. Whatever it was that had struck it had passed completely through it. There were open wounds on its underside and back. They would heal quickly, but it would require resources the fetus growing inside it needed.

Chapter 29

Summer, 1956

Erickson stared at Dave with a newfound respect for the man. Longo had seen the creature, drawn his revolver, and gotten a shot off before he had even realized what was happening. "How did you know it was there?" he asked.

"I don't know, I just knew. Maybe it's because I've got a history with it, or maybe it's because it just didn't feel right. Did you notice the jays stopped calling, and the woods got a little too quiet?"

Erickson shook his head. *I've got to get back to the city. Jays stopped calling? Woods got too quiet? What the hell is he talking about?*

"I doubt we'll get another chance today, but we can try," Longo said. "Let's keep walking."

They walked as far as the trestle, keeping to the bank where they could, drifting away from it when they had to. When they got there, Longo stared at the stone abutment and knew he didn't have a snowball's chance in hell of climbing it without a ladder. He had done it when he was young-er and thinner, but with the gut he was carrying now, he'd never be able to hug the wall like he had then.

"You want to climb up and take a look?" he asked Erickson.

"How the hell am I supposed to get up there?" Erickson asked, obviously intimidated by the fifteen feet of blank stone wall.

"I'll boost you up most of the way, and you should be able to climb the rest of the way on your own."

"I don't think so," Erickson told him. "Next time we can bring a ladder if you really want to get up there."

Longo stood in front of the abutment wishing there was a way to get to the top. It really provided an excellent view up and down the river, and a lot had happened back here in '39. He didn't tell Erickson that because the man was already teetering on the edge. If he pushed him any further, he'd be useless. Less than useless really, he'd be dangerous. At this point he was hoping they didn't find the oniare—the thing could carry him off and Erickson would still be trying to figure out what was happening. He was going to have to tell Miller he needed someone else for this.

* * *

The Chief just shook his head when Dave told him that Erickson wasn't cut out for looking for the oniare. "He's fine in town, but he's lost in the woods. I guess I'd be the same way in some big city, but I need someone else to work with, or I'm not going looking for it again."

"Then I guess it will have to be me. I don't want to bring anyone else in on this unless I have to. Erickson said you took a shot at it, is that right?"

"Yeah, but I missed. It was too far away for a pistol, but I couldn't pass up the chance of getting lucky. And the damn thing pissed me off. It was stalking us. I could feel it. I knew it was out there, but except for that one time it let me see it, I might as well have been as blind as Erickson."

"Okay, we can try again tomorrow, and this time, I'll go with you," Miller told him.

* * *

After the water had exploded next to its head, the oniare stayed in the shadows on the opposite bank and followed the men from a safe distance. It could reach them in seconds if one of them approached the water alone. Where there were no shadows, or the water was too shallow, it waited until the men were out of sight, and then it rushed past those places until it found them again. When they left the river and were out of sight for several minutes, it swam to the place it had seen the young one. Perhaps that one would be there again.

The place was deserted when the oniare got there, but it waited in the shadows for the two men to arrive at the bank. If they did, and one of them approached the water, it would grab him.

The men did arrive. They came near the bank, but neither man had approached the water. The oniare left, hoping to find something at the lake. If it couldn't find a host, it would feed on snakes and fish and anything else unlucky enough to cross its path.

Chapter 30

June, 2014

Ryan pulled into the gas station on the corner. It was a Mobil now. He couldn't remember what it had been when he lived here. Maybe a Texaco? He seemed to remember a sign with a flying red horse. He was surprised and pleased to see gas was forty cents a gallon cheaper in Vermont than it had been in Connecticut. He pulled the release for the gas cover and started to walk to the pump when he was met by a kid in a Mobil shirt with "*Jimmy*" stitched across the right breast pocket.

"Fill it up?" the kid asked as he reached for the nozzle.

"Uh, yeah," Ryan replied, wondering what was going on.

The kid saw the look on his face and then glanced at the Connecticut plates. "We still pump it for you here at Sonny's. I guess we're one of the last stations around to do that. You want regular or premium?"

"Regular," Ryan told him, and then got back in the car and waited for the kid to finish. When he was done, Ryan paid with a credit card and was on his way. *That was easy,* he thought. *Why the hell don't we have service like that in Connecticut? And why do we pay an extra forty cents a gallon to pump our own?*

As he drove down Main Street, he got another shock—the town had shrunk. The old houses he had always thought of as huge were smaller than the older houses back in Metta-basset. The distance between downtown and the elementary school that he remembered as a being so long was just two blocks. The west side was unchanged because it was a sheer rock wall at least fifty feet tall, and the east side was also the same as it had been. It was like a page out of time.

The elementary school was a different story. He remembered it as two-story brick building with high ceilings and windows that had been built in the early 1900s. He had spent hours on the blacktop basketball court as a teen, and recesses on the small dirt playground with two seesaws and a set of swings. There had been two additions since then. One was a two-story brick structure built onto the south side, with classrooms and what appeared to be a gym on the end. Another brick addition had been added off the back of the original section. The playground had been paved and was now a parking lot. Everywhere he looked, the ghost of the Poquonock that occupied his mind peeked out from behind the new, unfamiliar one he was faced with now.

The high school was more of the same. Several additions had been added, one of them on the site of the old baseball field. New athletic fields now filled an area that had been woods before.

Finally, when he couldn't put if off any longer, he headed toward The Back Beach. Along the way, he would drive past his old house and the house Bran had lived in. They were both on the last road in the development. Both houses backed up against the woods.

From the front, his house hadn't changed at all. When he looked at the side, however, the changes that had been made were apparent. An air conditioner stuck out of the attic window; when he lived there, that attic had been unfinished. It was an oven in the summer and an icebox in the winter. He remembered escaping up there to read comic books and the Hardy Boys. Now it was living space, and he could see that the back side of it had been dormered. This alone would have almost doubled the eight-hundred square feet of living space his family had shared. There was also an addition off the back, more added living space. He was impressed; a kid growing up there now could actually have his own bedroom.

The road to The Back Beach was at the end of the street, and it beckoned. He sat behind the wheel for a full five minutes, staring at it before he slipped the car from park to drive and crept toward it at a whopping five miles an hour. As soon as his tires left the paved street and crunched on the gravel of the dirt road, his hands started shaking and he felt sick to his stomach. After another fifty feet, and he was sweating in spite of the air conditioning; he could feel it on his brow and dripping down his side from his armpits. After another ten feet, he slammed on his brakes and skidded to a stop like he had done so many times before on his bike.

The shakes didn't stop until he had done a quick K-turn and was headed back to Connecticut.

Chapter 31

Summer, 1939

Dave Longo was obsessed with destroying the creature he had seen come out of the water to attack Chuck Turcott. He spent most of his waking hours near the river, or thinking of ways to find and kill it. "I'm thinking of buying a boat and motor so we can search for it," he told Turcott as they surveyed the river from the top of the trestle.

Turcott threw a stone in the water before answering. "Don't do that. The lake is a good idea, but I don't like the thought of being out on it in a boat."

"Why not? We could search a lot of places we'd never see from the shore."

"I still don't like it. We'd be putting ourselves in its environment. We'd have water all around us and no way to reach land if we had to."

"We could still do it, but we'd need to be *really* careful," Dave insisted. "And after what happened at the trestle, I don't see *that* being a problem."

"If we do this, we're going to need another person. Two of us will not be enough," Turcott told him.

"Why not? We did okay before."

"One guy will sit in the back and work the motor—that will be me. We need two guys to keep an eye on the water and be ready to help if the oniare attacks us. If you were sitting in the prow and I was operating the motor, it could grab you and haul you overboard before I could get to you or a gun."

"Good idea, but who do we get? The Chief and I can't both be out here."

Turcott hesitated before he answered. "My brother is the only one I can think of that I'd trust my life with."

"You have a brother? I didn't know that."

"Why would you? I'll have to drive over and talk to him tomorrow."

"Drive over and talk to him? Where does he live?"

"St. Albans"

"Why not just call him?"

"Two reasons," Turcott answered. "Neither one of us has a phone, and it's going to take some convincing to get him to come."

"Does he know about the oniare?"

"Yes, it's why he left Poquonock. My father wouldn't let him go with him when he fought the oniare. He thinks one of us could have followed him if I had been there. He blames me because I wasn't there to help," Turcott told him.

* * *

Turcott was filled with anxiety as he drove to St. Albans. *Will he let me in? Will he even talk to me? The last time I tried, he ignored me like I wasn't there. But he has to. I need to kill this thing once and for all.*

When he finally stood outside his brother's door, he was still unsure of what he was going to say when he finally faced him. They hadn't seen each other in twenty years. Matt might turn him away, but he had to try. He was standing in front of the door, frozen by indecision, when it suddenly opened and he was standing face to face with his twin.

"You," was all Matt said when he saw Chuck.

"Yes, me. Can I come in?"

"Why?"

And there it was, the question he had been dreading. He had been agonizing about it during the drive over here. His heart was pounding when he managed to blurt out, "Because the oniare's back, and I want you to help me kill it."

Matt didn't say anything, but he stepped back to allow his brother to enter. Then he led him to the kitchen and motioned for him to sit. "Tell me about it," he said when they were both sitting down at the table.

"It showed up last week and killed a stranger who had come to town. The Chief of Police found his clothes by the side of the river, so he thinks the man was bathing when the oniare got him."

"Why come to me?" Matt asked. Chuck could hear the evident contempt in his voice.

"Because I thought you would like a chance to kill this thing. And because you're the one person I could think of who I would trust with my life because I know you want to kill it as badly as I do."

"So, no one else is hunting this with you?"

"Two men: the Chief of Police, and his patrolman, Dave Longo. Longo has already been attacked by it. He saved my life when it attacked me."

"If you and these men are already hunting it, why do

you need my help?" Matt said.

"I don't *need* your help, but I'd like to have it. I thought you might want a chance to help kill this thing … and, like I said, I trust you."

Chuck was ready for his brother to turn him down, but he didn't. "Tell me everything," Matt said as he got up from the table and went to the sink to make coffee.

"A fisherman found the first body hung up on a fallen tree. When Longo tried to retrieve it, the oniare grabbed his leg. He managed to free himself with the help of the Chief, but he wound up with five long claw marks that required over a hundred stitches to close.

"The second one the oniare took was a twenty-year-old who had been drinking with friends by the river. When his friends left him there, he was drunk, but alive. The Chief found his body in Cooper Lake and brought it back to a trestle the lumber company had started to build across the river. He stayed with the body while the man who was with him when he found it went to tell Longo. The oniare attacked him while he waited." Turcott didn't tell his brother that Miller had drifted off, and that's why he had almost gotten himself killed. "He got two shots off at it with a revolver, but he missed."

Turcott stopped his narration while Matt poured coffee into two mugs. "You still take it with milk and sugar, or have you learned to drink it black, like a man?" his brother asked.

Turcott preferred his coffee with milk and sugar, but he said, "Black," because he knew it would please Matt to know Chuck had given in on this particular point. When Matt smiled and placed the cup in front of him, Chuck knew his brother had made it extra strong just to test him. When he took his first sip, it was all he could do not to cringe.

"So, tell me how this Longo fellow saved your life."

Turcott took a second sip of coffee before answering. "I

was setting traps for it in the river. I staked them to the bank and then attached them to a tree using a steel wire. I was hoping it would trip the trap and the wire would hold it. Once the traps were set, I was going to sit on the bank and attract it by throwing stones in the water."

Matt shook his head when he heard this. "And you thought this would work?"

"They were steel traps and, yes, I *hoped* it would work. Anyway, I thought it was worth a try. But I wasn't stupid about it; I had Longo cover me with Dad's old thirty-aught-six. The oniare attacked me when I was setting the third trap. It would have had me, too, if the first one hadn't snared it. It stopped it just before the thing reached me. It almost pulled the trap free, but it held just long enough for Longo to put a slug in it. As soon as that happened, the oniare fled back to the river, but not without leaving these in my trap," Turcott told him, and placed the creature's claws on the table.

Matt looked at the claws and swore, "Son-of-a-bitch, and you say this Longo put a slug in it?"

"Yes, so it's wounded. Now we have to go find it and kill it. Will you help us?"

Matt picked one of the claws off the table and ran his finger along the edge until he got to the tip. "Of course. You knew I would. Now tell me how you intend to do this."

Chapter 32

Summer, 1956

Ryan shook his head as he retrieved the bow and arrows from where he had stashed them. "Man, now I have to sneak these back into the house. I had enough trouble getting them out. Now I have to do it again."

"Why not just leave them here? No one will find them."

"Are you crazy? I'm not leaving my bow in the woods overnight." Ryan was surprised Bran would even suggest it.

"What if we stayed with them? We could camp out. You could keep them in the tent. You think your mom would let you do that?" Bran asked.

"My mom would, but what about yours? She's the one you have to convince."

"My mom will if she knows your mom says you can, so let's ask your mom first," Bran told Ryan.

* * *

When Ryan and Bran burst through the back door, Ryan immediately blurted out, "Hey, Mom, Bran and me want to camp out tonight."

"Bran and I want to camp out tonight," she corrected him, as he knew she would. It was all part of the plan to get her to say yes. Hit her with the request and then give her something else to think about.

"Yeah, well can we?"

"Yeah, Missus Lowell, can we?" Bran chimed in, giving her one more thing to deal with.

"Dad would let us, so can we?" Ryan said, playing the guilt card.

It was times like these that she wished her husband had a nine-to-five job instead of one that took him out of the house all week. "I guess so," she said, "but only in the back yard. Stay out of the woods."

"Ah, Mom," Ryan whined.

"No whining, it's the backyard or nothing," she shot back at him.

"Okay, we'll stay in the back yard," Ryan agreed, his voice practically dripping with disappointment, even though he was getting what he wanted.

"Thanks, Missus Lowell," Bran said on their way out the door. Phase one of their plan was complete. Now for phase two.

* * *

"Hey, Mom, Ryan and I are going to camp out in his backyard tonight. His mom said it was okay," Bran announced when they were at his house. "Please, Mom," Bran pleaded.

"We'll be fine, Missus Liotti. It's just in my backyard.

We've got a tent, and we can come inside if we have to," Ryan pitched in.

Helen Liotti looked from Bran to Ryan, and even though she wanted to say no, wanted to keep him home and safe, she also felt pressured to let him do what other boys his age were doing. But other boys his age had fathers, and their mothers had husbands. All she had was Bran.

"Oh, all right," she finally agreed. "But you don't leave until after dinner. I haven't seen you all day."

"Great," Bran answered, and then asked if Ryan could stay for supper.

"We're just having burgers and corn on the cob. Is that all right with you?" she asked Ryan.

"Yes, ma'am," he answered. "We're having beans and franks, and that's not good if you're sleeping in a tent."

"All right." she laughed. "Go ask your mom if it's okay."

"Okay," Bran agreed. "We'll be back after we set the tent up." Then they were out the door, running back to Ryan's house.

They set the tent up facing the brick fireplace Ryan's family used for cookouts. That way they could have a fire to sit in front of while they made their plans for the next day. When the bow, arrows, hatchet, slingshot, bag of marbles, and Bran's knife were safely hidden in the back under Ryan's sleeping bag, they went back to Bran's for dinner.

* * *

"Stand back," Bran said, then tossed the wooden match onto the pile of lighter fluid-soaked sticks and branches he had placed in the fireplace. As soon as the match hit the pile, a loud *whoosh* filled the air and flames shot three feet into the sky. Bran jumped back, stumbled over Ryan's feet, and fell on his butt.

"I think you used a little too much starter fluid," Ryan said when he managed to stop laughing.

"I guess so," Bran answered sheepishly, and then he started laughing, too. They both stopped when Ryan's mom called from the house, "Ryan, what did you do? Are you boys all right out there?"

"We're okay, Mom, Bran just used a little too much starter fluid to start the fire," Ryan called back.

"Well, be careful, boys. I don't want anyone to get hurt, and I don't want to have to call the fire department either."

"We will, Mom."

"We will, Missus Lowell," the boys called back, and then started laughing all over again. When they finally stopped, they both sat silently in front of the fire watching the flames dance. Neither one was quite ready to talk about what they were planning for tomorrow.

"Let's roast some marshmallows," Ryan suggested when the fire had burned down to coals.

"Okay," Bran answered, and stuck a marshmallow on the end of the birch stick he had already stripped of its bark. He held it over the coals, and when it started to blister and turn a golden brown he slowly turned it until the entire marshmallow was toasted. Sugary goo stuck to the tip of the stick as he plucked it off and ate it.

Bran tried not to watch as Ryan lowered his marshmallow so close to the coals that it caught fire. He hated the way Ryan did it, letting the marshmallow burn until it was black and crusty. Then he would blow on it until it was cool enough to eat it right off the stick. Bran had tried it once and almost burned his mouth. It was also disgusting; the crusty shell tasted like burnt paper ... yuck.

"How about a soda?" Ryan asked as he dug into the cooler his mom had packed for them.

"Sure, what have you got?" Bran asked, even though he knew it was going to be either orange or root beer.

He was surprised when Ryan said, "Hey, there's a Coke in here. You want that?"

"Yeah, I'll take the Coke," Bran answered, and thought, *thank you, Missus Lowell.* She must have stuck it in there just for him. Ryan *only* drank orange or root beer—kids' drinks. He had outgrown them, but Coke, well, Coke was cool. Cherry Coke was even better, but you could only get that at the counter at Woolworth's. Man, he wished they'd put that stuff in a bottle.

After consuming a whole bag of marshmallows and two sodas each, Ryan dropped another log on the fire to keep it going. Neither of them said anything until it burst into flames. Surprisingly, it was Ryan who spoke first. "I think we should do it at The Rock."

"Why The Rock? I was thinking we should do it at the trestle," Bran answered.

Ryan shook his head and tossed a twig onto the coals and waited for it to catch fire. "No, The Rock. I want to be shooting down at it, and I don't want to be on the trestle. Remember what happened there the last time?"

Bran didn't answer, but Ryan knew his friend was thinking back to his encounter with the creature.

"At The Rock, we can see it coming, and we can get away quick if we have to. I don't think it would be able to come after us there. It can't dig those claws into the rock."

"Yeah, I guess you're right," Bran answered. He had to admit that Ryan was a thinker, a planner, whereas he was more of a "just do it and think about the consequences later" kind of guy. That was probably not a good idea in this case.

"You remember what Mister Longo said about the stones, how the noise attracts it when you throw them in the water? I think we should bring a bunch with us. We should get them before we get to The Rock. We can get them at the sand pit."

"Good idea," Bran had to agree again.

"Anything else?" he asked, curious to see what else Ryan might have planned.

"Yeah, don't go anywhere near the water. That thing wants you, and it will kill you if it gets you. You have to promise me you'll stay on top of The Rock with me."

Bran thought for a minute, crossed his fingers behind his back, and finally agreed. "Okay, I'll stay on top of The Rock."

They sat in silence again, each lost in his own thoughts, until Bran finally asked, "What time is it?"

"Geez," Ryan said, using his flashlight to check his watch. "It's 12:30. We better get some sleep."

That proved to be easier said than done. Both boys were riding a sugar high from the marshmallows and soda, and they were nervous about facing the creature in the river. Ryan fell asleep first at 2:30, and Bran followed at 3:00.

* * *

"Knock, knock, you sleepy heads. Do you want breakfast?" Ryan heard his mom's voice and rolled over, wondering where he was. When he saw Bran sleeping on the other side of the tent with a dribble of drool coming from his open mouth, everything came rushing back at him. "What time is it?" he called as he shook Bran awake.

"It's 10:30. How long did you boys stay up last night?"

"What?" he answered, wide awake now.

"Did she say 10:30?" Bran asked, sitting up and rubbing

the sleep out of his eyes.

"Yeah, what are we going to do?" Ryan hissed.

"Did you say something, dear?" his mother asked.

"Uh, yeah," he answered, "we'll be in in a minute."

"No," Bran mouthed, and elbowed him in the side.

"Yes," Ryan hissed. "If we say no and leave for the woods, she'll know we're up to something. We can still go after we eat."

"All right, then, pancakes and sausage will be ready in about ten minutes. Make sure you clean up before you sit down to eat. And, Bran, you go home and tell your mom you're okay, and you're having breakfast over here. She called about you this morning, and I told her you were still sleeping."

"Okay, Missus Lowell," Bran answered, and ran home to tell his mother he was fine.

"You boys make sure you take the tent down and put everything away before you go running off in those woods," Ryan's mom said as they were finishing their breakfast.

"We were hoping we could sleep out again tonight, weren't we, Bran?" Ryan said as he put the last sausage on his plate.

"Un-huh," Bran agreed around a mouthful of pancakes.

"I don't know … You boys were up pretty late last night," she said.

"We'll go to sleep early this time, I promise," Ryan said.

"Me, too, and this time no marshmallows or soda. That's what kept us awake," Bran told her.

"How many marshmallows did you eat?" she asked.

Ryan looked down at the table before answering. "The whole package, and we each had two sodas."

"No wonder you boys couldn't get to sleep! If you stay out tonight, no snacks and no soda. You can have sandwiches and water, that's it."

"Great, thanks, Mom," Ryan said, and bolted toward the door. Bran gulped down the last of his milk and just managed to reach the screen door before it slammed shut.

Mrs. Lowell stared after them and then realized she had just given them permission to stay out another night.

Ryan waited for Bran to catch up, then said, "Let's go tell your mom we're sleeping out in the tent again tonight."

"Okay, but then we have to go find the creature," Bran told him.

Ryan stopped and looked at his friend. "It's too late for that. We'll go tomorrow morning."

"What do you mean it's too late? We have plenty of time."

"No, we don't. Mister Longo and Mister Erickson are looking for it, and we don't know where they are. We could walk right up to them carrying all our stuff. They'd bring us home and we'd be grounded. Besides, it's a hot day; there's going to be a lot of people at the river today. We need to get there early."

Bran didn't like it, but he knew Ryan was right. "Fine, what else do you want to do?"

"Practice with the hunting arrows. They're heavier than my target arrows."

"Good idea, and I can practice throwing the hatchet," Bran agreed.

Bran started to go into the tent, but Ryan stopped him. "Wait, let me check with my mom. I'll wave when you can take the stuff to the woods."

"Okay," Bran agreed. Once he was in the tent, he realized once again that Ryan thought this stuff out a lot better than he did. He had just gathered everything up when he saw Ryan waving from the back door. He was out of the tent and headed for the woods in a flash. He didn't stop running till he got to the fort. He knew Ryan would know where he had gone.

* * *

While Bran and Ryan were eating pancakes, Chuck Turcott was consuming the biggest breakfast he had eaten in years. He had a plateful of scrambled eggs, six slices of bacon, two sausage patties, and a huge mug of black coffee. He hadn't had a drink since he woke up hung over the morning after the boys visit. Sitting beside him on the table were nine yellowed claws and two hunting knives. The knives had been dulled by inattention and age, but he had fixed that. Now they were free of tarnish and razor sharp because they had work to do.

* * *

"Let's go check out all the places you've seen it this time," Miller told Longo over coffee at Guy's.

"Why?" Longo wanted to know. "You were there the last time."

"I just want to get a feel for the river. I haven't been back there in years. I need to be able to picture it in my mind."

That's probably a good idea, Longo thought. Except for the ball field and The Back Beach, the river hadn't changed that much since they had hunted the oniare back in '39. "The first place we'll be going to, then, is The Rock. That's where Ryan Lowell and Brandon Liotti saw it for the first time."

"The *first* time?" the Chief said, quick to pick up on what Longo had said.

Longo waited while the waitress refilled his coffee cup before answering. "Yeah, the first time. Brandon saw it again at the trestle. He was alone then." He didn't mention that the thing had almost caught the kid.

"It was in the river between The Logs and the beach when I took those two shots at it. Erickson never did see it, but it spooked the hell out of him."

"Has anyone else seen it?" Miller wanted to know.

"Not that I know of."

"Right," the Chief said, and slid his coffee cup away from him. "Let's get started."

Dave nodded in agreement, left thirty cents on the counter for their coffee along with a quarter for a tip, and led the way to his car. Guy had tried to tell Longo that the coffee was free for the Police Department, but Dave still insisted on paying.

* * *

Miller and Longo stood together at the top of The Rock looking at the spot where Weiss had found McCauley's body and the oniare had slashed Dave's leg back in '39. "I can't believe we're down here doing this again," Miller said as he watched a muskrat swim across the cove and disappear into the bank on the opposite shore. "Where'd the kids see it, exactly?"

Longo pointed to the spot. "Right there, where the water's deepest. That's where kids dive from when they swim here."

"That's where I used to dive from, too," Miller said. "I'd dive in and try to swim all the way across underwater. There used to be a sandy spot you could stand up on near the other bank, but mostly it was all gravel and weeds."

"The oniare's not here. That muskrat never would have shown itself if it was. Let's go back to the beach," Longo said, climbing down off The Rock and back to the car.

"See that big oak tree, the one with the broken branch?" Longo said, pointing across the river.

"Yeah," Miller answered.

"Okay, directly in line with that oak, and about ten feet from the bank, that's where it was when I shot at it. If I had taken my time to aim better, I might have hit the damn thing."

"Yeah, and if you *had* taken your time it might have been gone before you could get a shot off and you'd be kicking yourself in the ass about that," the Chief replied.

"Yeah, you're probably right," Longo admitted. "Let's take a ride down to the trestle."

"You ever climb that thing when you were a kid?" Longo asked when they got there.

"No," Miller replied. "I was never one for the woods. I was only down here once before the oniare killed the Billings kid. I was here with a bunch of other kids to party. I don't remember who, but after a few beers, someone suggested we all go skinny dipping. Everyone laughed until Sue Shea said it sounded like a good idea. There were six of us, three guys and three girls. We stripped down naked and slipped into the water. Damn it was cold, but with three naked girls splashing and laughing in the moonlight, I wasn't about to complain. The water came to our waists, so we were getting an eyeful, but the girls weren't seeing what they wanted to see. I damn near died when Donna Tripp grabbed my dick and squeezed it under water. We went together for a year after that before she moved to Albany."

Longo chuckled, and then said, "The only place I went skinny dipping was at Echo Rock, and I was always alone. Guess I missed out on something there."

"Where's Echo Rock?" Miller asked.

"About half-way down Cooper Lake. There's a dirt road that used to go there, but it's so washed out now that the only way to get to it is to walk, or ride a bike like the kids do. I imagine some of them still go down there, but it's pretty far. Maybe we should check it out."

"Let's not. Let's just stick to the river for now. You got that bag of rocks you talked about?"

"In the trunk, along with the 12-gauge from the office," Longo told him.

"A shotgun? Wouldn't a rifle be better? You have to get pretty close to use a shotgun," Miller said.

"I intend to," Longo answered.

Chapter 33

Summer, 1939

Chuck and Matt Turcott rode in silence for the first ten miles of the trip back to Poquonock. When he could stand it no longer, Chuck broke the silence by asking, "Do you still blame me for Dad's death?"

"If you had been there ..." Matt started to say, but Chuck cut him off.

"If I had been there, he would've done the same thing, and you know it. He wouldn't have let me help fight that thing any more than he let you."

"But you wouldn't have let him; you would have fought it anyway. I would have just stood there and watched."

So that's what this has been about for all these years, Chuck finally realized. His brother wasn't mad at him; he was mad at himself.

"No, I wouldn't have. I defied him in the little things; I snuck out at night, stole cigarettes out of his pack, but his stories about the oniare terrified me. If I had been there, it probably would have killed me, too. At least you got away. I would have stood there like a lamb waiting for slaughter."

"I don't believe that," Matt told him.

"Oh, believe it. For years after he died, I hated myself for not being there, but still thanked God every day that I wasn't. When I found out the thing was back, I realized it was a chance to redeem myself by killing it … and that's what we're going to do. Come hell or high water, that's what we're going to do—you and me."

"Why did you wait so long to ask for my help?" Matt asked.

Chuck took his eyes off the road for a minute and looked into his brother's. "Because I was afraid you'd turn me down … no, it was because I didn't want to risk your life, too. That thing killed Dad when I wasn't there. I didn't want to bring you back and take the chance it might kill you, too."

Matt fingered the oilcloth sitting on the seat beside them before replying. "Well, this time we kill it."

"What exactly have you got in there?" Chuck asked, eyeing the bundle.

Matt carefully unwrapped the package and drew out two long knives. "These were Dad's. I got them from the river when I finally got up enough courage to go back for them."

Chuck pulled over, stopped the car, and stared at the knives his brother was holding. They were a matched set. Each had an eight-inch blade with a razor-sharp cutting edge on one side and a serrated edge on the other. He hadn't seen them since his father had been killed. He thought they were lost forever.

"This one's yours," Matt said, and handed him the one with *Chuck* burned into the handle. He kept the one named *Matt* for himself.

Chuck took the blade by the handle, careful not to cut himself when he did. Tears came to his eyes and he had to pull over. "I thought these were lost," he managed to say when he got his emotions under control.

* * *

Longo looked up to see Chuck Turcott walk into the police station ... and then he watched him walk in again. *What the hell,* he thought, and then remembered Chuck said he was going to get his brother to help. He had neglected to say it was his *twin* brother. It was like Chuck, whichever one of them *was* Chuck, was standing next to a mirror. Both men were short, but wiry. Each had his long hair worn in a braid. Each had a touch of grey at the temples. Both were wearing jeans and a white T-shirt. The only difference he could see between them was the one on the left was wearing a big Indian-head belt buckle.

"Chuck ...?"

"Dave," Indian-head belt buckle answered, then turned and said, "This is my brother, Matt."

Longo stood and extended his hand. "Nice to meet you, Matt. I wish it could have been under better circumstances. How the hell am I supposed to tell you two apart?"

"I'm the smart one," Chuck told him.

"And I'm the good-looking one," Matt said. "Now, let's talk about how we're going to kill this thing."

"Before we do that," Chuck said, "I think we should tell Dave how Dad killed one and what happened when he did." Then he looked at his brother and added, "This is Matt's story to tell. I wasn't there when it happened."

Matt sat down, looked around, saw the coffee pot and hot plate, and said, "How about a cup of coffee first? I'm going to need a minute." When he was ready, he told them what had happened.

"We ran the Grange back then. It was a place for people

to get their mail, buy just about anything, or just sit and talk. Charlie Moore came into the store, talking about a creature in the river. Said it was like a big snake, but it had hands and a nasty-looking face with ice-blue eyes. Charlie was pretty much the town drunk, and everyone ignored him, everyone but Dad. He took Charlie aside and got the whole story out of him. I had just turned sixteen, so this was back in '85. Poquonock wasn't even a town back then. We were still part of West Milton.

"Charlie saw the oniare from the railroad trestle. Said the thing was swimming around down there like a big old carp, but it was bigger than any damn carp he had ever seen. He threw a stone at it, and when it looked up and saw him, it stopped moving, and then just disappeared. Dad told him he should just keep quiet about it because people would never believe him and he didn't want to become the town's laughing stock."

Matt stopped here, picked up his cup, and asked Longo if he could have a refill.

"Sure," Dave answered, and got up to get the pot. After refilling Matt's cup, he held up the pot and offered Chuck a refill.

Chuck looked into his cup. It was still half full. "No thanks, I'm good."

Matt continued. "I told Dad we should wait until Chuck got home and the three of us could go after it, but he wouldn't wait. 'It's my job to kill it, not Chuck's, not yours. If I wait, it could be gone. I need to go now. You watch the store,' he said. And I did; I stayed and watched the store."

"What else could you have done?" Chuck asked.

"I could have closed the store and went with him," Matt answered.

"You think that now, but he would have whipped you

right there on Main Street if you had done that. You know that," Chuck told him.

"So who went with him?" Longo asked.

Matt looked at Chuck, and then Longo, before answering. "No one. He went by himself."

"By himself? He killed one of those things by himself?"

"Yes, but it killed him, too," Chuck answered. "When I got back to the store, Matt told me what had happened. It was almost closing time anyway, so we closed up early and went looking for him."

Matt picked the story back up from there. "We went to the train trestle where Charlie said he saw it. When we got there, we saw Dad floating face down in the river. I don't remember how we got down the embankment; I only know that when we got to him, he was already dead. The oniare had torn him apart with its claws. His shirt was shredded, he had deep cuts on his back and chest, and his throat was torn out."

"We found the oniare, most of it anyway, a few feet away. It was cut up as bad as Dad, and its head was hanging by a few threads of flesh and bone," Matt continued. "We cut it the rest of the way off, and later we burned it. We dragged the body out into the current and let the river take it."

"What about your father?" Longo asked.

"Matt stayed with him and I went back to the store for a blanket and some rope. When I came back, we wrapped him in the blanket, tied it so it wouldn't unwrap, and carried him home. We buried him the next day."

"What about your mother?" Longo asked.

"We never knew our mother. She died two years after we were born." Chuck told him.

"What did you do after that?"

"I left," Matt answered. "But not before I went back and

found Dad's knives. After that, I just couldn't stay here."

"I left, too, but I came back. I've been here ever since, waiting and watching for the oniare to return. And now, here it is."

"But your father killed it," Longo told them.

Matt looked Longo in the eyes and said. "It's another one. There's always another one."

Chapter 34

Summer, 2014

Ryan's heart didn't stop hammering in his chest until he was on the highway heading back to Connecticut. Just before he got to the Massachusetts border, he was chastising himself for running away. In Brattleboro, he realized he had a decision to make: keep driving on I-91 back to Connecticut, or turn around and go back to Poquonock. He wanted to go back, he really did, but he didn't know if he could, so he decided to get off the highway and get a room. He'd sleep on it and make that decision in the morning.

He slept, but his slumber was filled with dreams of Bran and the oniare. In them, both the oniare and Bran beckoned to come to the river—the oniare because it wanted him, Bran because he wanted him to kill the monster. In the dream that shocked him awake, the oniare had lunged out of the river to grasp him with its claws. Still groggy with sleep, he thought he saw Bran standing next to the bed holding his hand out to him. Then the vision faded and he realized where he was, and that it had all been a horrible dream.

Chapter 35

Summer, 1956

"Two nights in a row? I'm not sure I like that," Bran's mother said when the boys told her of their plans.

"Aww, Mom! Ryan's mom said it was okay, and we're right in his back yard."

She held out through five minutes of begging before giving in. "Okay, but only if you boys eat dinner here tonight. And you," she said, pointing to Bran. "Take a bath after dinner. I'm not letting you out of this house smelling like you do now."

Bran stuck his nose down his T-shirt, sniffed, and said, "What's wrong with the way I smell?"

His mom wrinkled her nose and told him he smelled like a campfire.

* * *

They were sitting on Ryan's front porch tossing pebbles

at a tin can when Bran said, "This is boring. Let's *do* something!"

"Sure, as long as we stay out of the woods and away from the river," Ryan told him.

"You got any money?" Bran asked.

"Have *you* got any?" Ryan returned. He didn't want to admit he did, only to find out Bran didn't.

"I've got fifty cents, my allowance. How about you?"

"I've got some change on my dresser. My dad left it for the ice cream truck."

"How much?"

"Fifty cents, ten cents for each day," Ryan answered.

"Okay, we've got a dollar. Let's go to Mackey's and get cherry cokes and see if they have any new comics."

Ryan didn't like the idea of spending all his money in one day, but the allure of new comics proved to be too much. "Okay," he finally agreed.

The bike ride to Mackey's only took ten minutes, but that was because Bran was leading the way. He never just rode on his bike; it was always a race to him. Ryan had long since given up trying to slow him down ... he was happy to just keep him in sight.

When Ryan reached Mackey's, Bran's bike was standing on its kickstand outside and he was already sitting at the counter ordering two cherry cokes. Ryan took the stool next to him. Within a minute, Mackey put a cherry coke in front of each of them. "What's this?" he asked. "I didn't order a Coke."

"Your friend ordered for the both of you," Mackey told him.

Ryan winked at Mackey and then said, "Then he can pay for it. I didn't want a Coke. I wanted an egg cream."

Bran looked at his friend in surprise. Egg creams were

fifteen cents. "We said cherry cokes; you never said you wanted an egg cream."

"*You* said cherry cokes. You never asked me what I wanted."

"One egg cream, coming up," Mackey said, playing along.

"But, what about …" Bran started to say and then realized Ryan was pulling his leg. "Dick-head," he said, and punched Ryan in the arm.

"Ow," Ryan said, but he was laughing when he did.

"I think he got you," Mackey told Bran before going off to wait on another customer.

When they were done with their cherry cokes, Ryan slid off his stool and looked toward the back of the store where the comics were displayed on wooden racks. "Let's see if there are any new ones in."

They found two new Supermans, a Batman, an Aquaman, a Green Lantern, and a Flash. Ryan bought the Supermans and the Batman. Bran got the Aquaman, Green Lantern, and the Flash. It didn't matter who bought which ones because they swapped them back and forth on a weekly basis. They spent the next few hours in Bran's room reading them. Neither boy realized it, but Ryan's little trick had broken the tension. They were able to forget about the oniare for at least a few hours. They were debating whether Kryptonite could actually kill Superman, or just make him weak when Bran's mother called them to dinner.

Dinner turned out to be the hot dogs and beans they were going to have last night, but there was a plateful of corn on the cob to go with it. The boys wanted soda, too, but Mrs. Liotti insisted on milk instead, which was good because there was apple pie for dessert. Apple pie went much better with milk than with soda.

* * *

"We're going to get up early and go fishing, so we might not be here for breakfast," Ryan told his mom before they headed for the tent.

"Oh no, you don't. You come in for breakfast or you don't sleep out in that tent. You boys are getting a little too independent for me," Mrs. Lowell told them.

"Aww, Mom," Ryan replied, and was ready to argue when she said,

"No 'Aww, Moms'. You come in for breakfast or you don't sleep out."

"*Fine,*" he agreed, "but we'll be in *really* early. You might not be up yet."

"That's okay. You can have cereal. I'll leave it on the counter with some fruit. And I'd better find the empty bowls in the sink if you leave before I get up."

"Fine," he said again, and stomped out of the house.

"Watch and see how it's done," Ryan said as he piled twigs on top of some crumpled newspaper pages on the bottom of the fireplace. When he lit the paper, a small flame caught and quickly spread. In a minute the twigs were burning and he was starting to add some bigger sticks.

Bran looked at the growing fire and frowned. "Where's the fun in that? My way is a lot cooler." Then he quickly changed the subject. "So, we get up early, have breakfast, and go looking for that thing," he said as he stared into the fire.

"Crap," Ryan swore.

"What?"

"I forgot to practice with the hunting arrows."

"So take a few shots in the morning. You'll be fine," Bran

assured him.

Ryan wasn't so sure, and it worried him.

"You ever hear about the H-man?" Ryan asked as they stared into the flames.

"No," Bran answered. "Do I want to?"

Ryan didn't answer yes or no. He just started telling the story.

"The H-man is a guy who lived in the woods a long time ago. He had a cabin that he built himself. He hardly ever came out of the woods. He got his food by hunting and fishing. One night he woke up and found his cabin was on fire. He tried to get out, but he couldn't … not until the roof caved in on top of him. That's how he escaped, but he got burned really bad. When he healed up, he had horrible scars all over his body. One looked like a big H burned into his chest. That's why they call him the H-man."

"Cool," Bran said.

"Not cool," Ryan answered, "because he's still out there and he hates fires. If he sees a campfire with people sitting around it, he rushes in, kills all the people, and stomps the fire out."

"Ew, creepy," Bran said. "But, pretty good."

"Your turn. How about a ghost story?" Ryan told his friend and waited to see what Bran could come up with.

Bran was silent for several minutes before asking, "Do you believe in ghosts?"

"Sure. Doesn't everybody?" Ryan answered.

"No, I mean it. Do you really believe in ghosts?"

"I don't know," Ryan answered when he realized Bran was serious. "Do you?"

"I want to," Bran said as he stirred the coals of the fire with the stick he had used to roast marshmallows the night before.

The answer took Ryan by surprise. "Why?" he finally asked.

"Because if ghosts are real, I might get to see my dad again. I hardly remember him at all. But if I could see him just once ..." Bran said, and then fell silent.

"I guess ghosts could be real," Ryan told his friend. "I mean, I never believed monsters could be real until I saw one in the river."

"Yeah, me, too. But I don't think I'd want to be one." Then Bran lightened the mood by putting his flashlight under his chin and saying, "But if I ever am, I'm going to come back and haunt you. Bwa-ha-ha."

* * *

"Come on, Ryan, wake up," Bran said as he shook his friend's shoulder for what seemed like the tenth time. "We need to get going."

"What time is it?" Ryan mumbled as he tried to pull his sleeping bag over his head.

"Time to eat breakfast and get going."

Ryan started to roll away from Bran, and when he did, he rolled onto his bow and remembered exactly what they were going to do that day. That was all it took to snap him awake.

The first thing they did when they went into the kitchen was look at the time. It was 5:30. Ryan's mom was still sleeping, but they found Raisin Bran and bananas on the kitchen counter. There was also half a box of powdered donuts. The milk was in the fridge.

"Oh man, not Raisin Bran," Ryan said when he saw the box.

"What's wrong with Raisin Bran? I like it," Bran told him.

"Yeah, but it makes you fart, just like the beans. You were farting all night. Does your mom know they make you fart like that?"

"Of course, that's why we had them last night," Bran said, and as if on cue, he ripped one off as he reached for the box on the counter.

"Pig," Ryan said, and threw a banana at him.

"Get the milk and let's eat. We need to get out of here," Bran said, and started to shovel his cereal into his mouth. Normally, they would have cut the bananas up and put them on the cereal, but today they wolfed down their Raisin Bran and took the bananas and donuts with them in a paper bag.

Minutes later, the snacks were in Ryan's Army surplus backpack and they were headed into the woods armed with the bow and arrows, the sling shot, hatchet, Bran's hunting knife, and the optimism of youth. The thought that one of them could actually die never crossed their minds.

* * *

Turcott stepped out of the shower and examined himself, at least what he could, in the medicine cabinet mirror. What he saw was not encouraging. The fit, hard-bodied man that had fought the oniare back in 1939 was gone. In his place was a skinny old man with too little meat on his bones. Time and rye whiskey had seen to that. The only thing unchanged was his eyes. For a moment they were still filled with fire and an overpowering need to kill the nightmare that was back and hunting in the river ... again. But then, the fire went out and his shoulders sagged. *Who am I kidding? I'd only get myself killed and the oniare would have all of us. Someone else is going to have to kill this one.*

Chapter 36

Summer, 1939

Dave Longo and the Turcott twins met at Guy's Diner for breakfast. Chuck Turcott had a boat and trailer hooked up to the back of his 1932 Buick. Longo watched as Chuck drove in and was dismayed not to see a motor on the back of the boat. *What the hell? Does he expect us to row that thing up and down the river?*

"Where's the motor? You said you had one," Dave demanded when Chuck got out of the car.

"Don't worry, it's in the trunk along with the other stuff," Chuck told him. At least he assumed it was Chuck because he was driving. When they got out of the Buick, Longo was happy to see they were wearing different colored shirts. Chuck's was a white T-shirt, while Matt's was black.

"Let's go inside," Longo said. "We can talk in there. And breakfast is on the town, by the way."

The Turcott brothers each ordered eggs, pancakes, sausage, orange juice, and coffee. Longo asked for coffee and a slice of apple pie. Before the waitress could walk away, Chuck Turcott told her, "Bring Dave what we're having, along with that pie."

Longo started to say he never had a big breakfast, but Chuck said, "We may be out there all day. You need to eat."

"I guess you're right. Bring it on," he told the waitress.

As they ate, Chuck outlined the plan he and Matt had worked out the night before. "We're going to put the boat in at the trestle since it gives us access to most of the river and the lake. I'm going to work the motor. You and Matt are going to sit in front, one of you on each side. Dave, you can have the rifle. Matt, you'll have the shotgun."

Matt shook his head and held up his knife. "I'll have this."

"Right," Chuck agreed, "but you can also have the shotgun. If we can kill it, or wound it before it gets to one of us, nobody needs to get sliced up or killed. You've seen the claws on that thing. Dave, you'll also have my machete. I'll have your pistol and my spear. Everybody good with that?"

Longo and Matt nodded their agreement.

When they finished eating, Longo paid the bill and they met in the parking lot. "You riding with us, or taking your car?" Chuck asked him.

"I'll take my car—you never know, we could need it."

"Okay," Chuck agreed. "Why don't you follow me? Leave me enough room to back in toward the river when we get there. Then you can park in front of me."

Longo agreed and followed close behind until they left the paved road and Turcott's car and trailer started throwing up a rooster tail of dirt and stones. Dave had to back off a hundred yards to let the dust settle enough so it didn't cover his car or crack his windshield.

When Turcott reached the trestle, he pulled slightly past the turnoff and started backing the boat toward the water. He stopped when the trailer was still ten yards from the river.

Then he waited for Longo to park and join them.

"What now?" Longo asked when they were all standing near the boat.

"You're going to cover me from here. Matt's going to get on the trestle and watch for the oniare while I get the boat in the water. I don't want that thing coming out of the river and grabbing me while I'm getting the boat in."

Longo looked at the bare stone face of the trestle's abutment. "How's he supposed to get up there?" he wanted to know.

"With this," Chuck answered as he removed a step-ladder he had tied to the seats of the boat. It wouldn't reach all the way up, but it would get Matt high enough to where he could reach the top and pull himself up the rest of the way.

Matt took the ladder, placed it against the abutment, and climbed. When he reached the top, Chuck climbed the ladder and handed up the shotgun. "What have you got in this thing?" Matt asked.

"Double-0 Buck with a full choke," Chuck answered.

When Matt was at his place on the trestle and Longo was stationed on the bank, Chuck asked his brother, "Any sign of it?"

Matt shaded his eyes and looked up and down the river. Then he turned his attention to the area immediately around the trestle. "Nope, it's clear as far as I can see."

Chuck hooked the motor to the rear of the boat and backed the trailer up to the river. "Get ready, I'm sliding it in," he called, and slid the boat off the trailer and into the water. The current caught it, and the boat started to move downstream before he pulled it to shore with the rope tied to the bow.

"I'm going to get in first. Matt, you keep an eye on the river when I do. Once I'm in, you can come down while Dave keeps watch from the bank. Then Dave can get in, and then you. Once you're in, I want everyone to tie a rope around their waist, and then tie it to the seat. When we're all in place, we'll head downriver toward the lake."

"What's the rope for?" Longo wanted to know.

"It's a precaution. If the oniare manages to grab one of us and pull him overboard, it won't be able to drag him off. The rope will give us a way to get him back."

"Sounds like you're using us for bait," Matt told him.

"Anything that works," Chuck agreed, and climbed into the boat. When he took his seat in the back, he tied his own rope around his waist and attached it to a hole he had drilled in his seat.

Longo got in next and took his place in the bow. When he was seated and his rope was firmly anchored, Matt came aboard, slipped past him, and took up his place in the middle. Then, with everyone in place, Chuck yanked on the pull cord and started the motor. After backing to the center of the river, he aimed the bow downstream and they headed toward the lake.

Chuck let the current carry them slowly downstream, only using the motor to keep them centered between the banks. He and Matt scanned the water as they went, but they soon realized that was mostly useless. Unless they floated directly over it, or the creature's head poked above the surface, they had little hope of sighting it. When the water was shallow, they could actually see to the bottom in areas where the surface was shaded, but where it wasn't, the sun turned the river into a sparkling mirror. It looked like they were on a fool's errand, but they kept at it.

From time to time they passed fallen trees that poked above the river's surface. These were usually covered with eastern painted turtles that would plop into the water like little depth charges. Once, a muskrat swam across their path, swallows skimmed the surface chasing insects, frogs croaked — but there was no sign of the oniare.

When they reached the lake, the river widened. Now, a job that had seemed nearly impossible before seemed hopeless. From shore to shore the lake was at least a quarter of a mile wide, and it stretched two miles before it ended at the West Milton dam. The surface was choked in places with lily pads and water grasses; in others, where it was too deep, it was smooth as glass.

"Now what?" Longo asked with a touch of resignation in his voice.

"Now we keep looking," Matt answered.

Here, with hardly any current to drag the boat along, Chuck had to twist the motor's throttle control to keep them moving.

* * *

The oniare heard the noise from the boat's motor long before it reached the spot where it was lying on the lake's bottom in a forest of lily pad stems. The hand that the trap had damaged still ached, and the wound from the slug that had torn through it was still open, but those pains were nothing compared to the creature's need to find a host for the young one growing inside it.

Excited by the sound, the oniare rose slowly to the surface. Vibrations in the water told it exactly where the boat was even though it couldn't see it. The sun reflecting off the surface hid the boat from the oniare's eyes as effectively as it hid it from theirs. The oniare could wait, concealed in the lily pads, or make its way toward them. If they were in open water, there would be less cover and more of a chance of being seen, but the oniare was a hunter; waiting and watching were not in its nature.

The oniare studied the boat with three potential hosts from a distance. Any one of them would do. It would grab one, haul it from the boat, and drag it to the bottom. Once it had killed the host and implanted the fetus in its body, it would hide the body where no one would ever find it. But to do all that, it needed deep water.

The oniare waited as the boat slipped through the lily pads and grasses near where the river widened into the lake. When it finally passed through the shallow, weedy area and passed into a deeper part of the lake, the creature used its powerful tail to speed through the water toward it. The oniare stayed low, near the bottom, until it was nearly below the boat. Then, with one final flick of its tail, the creature launched itself up and out of the water. It grabbed the man in the rear of the boat and pulled him back into the lake. The whole thing was over in seconds. The attack was so quick and un-expected that the man was in the water before he had time to react. The oniare had its prey and was heading back to the bottom.

The host was struggling, trying to fight, but the oniare was in its habitat. As soon as they were far enough away from the others, the oniare would force the man's mouth open to allow the fetus to claw its way inside his throat. Then it would be free to return to the big lake to live out what years it might have left. Relief replaced the fear the oniare had been living with. Then something grabbed the man and the fear returned, and along with it—rage. It would not be denied again.

Chapter 37

Summer, 2014

Ryan looked in the bathroom mirror and made his decision. He was going back to Poquonock. There was no way he could live with himself or look at his reflection every day for the rest of his life if he didn't. With the decision made, his appetite, which had abandoned him when he fled Poquonock, returned with a vengeance. He knew the complimentary continental breakfast would never do. Instead, he packed up, checked out and drove to the Cracker Barrel he had seen when he got off the highway. Once there, he ordered Grampa's Country Fried Breakfast. He got two eggs over easy, grits, chicken fried steak with sawmill gravy, homemade buttermilk biscuits, and the hash brown casserole. A pot of black coffee and a glass of orange juice finished his order. He could almost hear his arteries crying for mercy when the waitress placed it in front of him.

When Ryan walked out of the Cracker Barrel, he was amazed at the difference in the day. Yesterday, everything had seemed dull and washed out; today, the trees were a vibrant green, the sky a dazzling blue, and the clouds impossibly white. He could taste summer in the air, smell it on the wind. He couldn't remember feeling this alive in decades. His euphoria faded as he drove back to Poquonock, but his resolve never faltered.

* * *

Ryan's heart rate increased again when he left the paved road, but he kept driving. He knew he would be okay if he could get past the spot where he had panicked the last time. He sped down the road, only slowing a bit when he fishtailed on the loose gravel. When he saw the ruts he had left in the soft shoulder when he had turned tail the day before, he took his foot off the gas and let the car slow to a saner pace.

Coasting to a crawl, Ryan looked for the old foundation that he and Bran had used for a fort in the summer of '56. *Where are you?* he thought as he passed by trees that had been no more than saplings back then. He finally gave up and parked along the side of the road. *I'll just have to get in there and find it.*

After he pushed through the undergrowth at the side of the road, the old growth woods he remembered emerged. Tall oaks shaded the forest floor, and ferns replaced the smaller trees and bushes that had blocked his view. The rocky ridge he remembered ran directly in front of him, and there was the cleft Bran and he had used to climb up and down it when they were feeling adventurous. *I passed it,* he thought, and turned left, thinking it should be no more than several hundred yards from where he stood. But once again, memory and reality were at odds, and he was amazed to find it less than fifty yards away.

He wasn't sure what he had expected, but it was not what he found. There was no sign of the secret hideaway he and Bran had built. Now it was nothing more than a ruin. The room they had turned into their fort was filled with the detritus of over fifty years of falling leaves and twigs. Someone had once used the rest of the old foundation as a dump. It was filled with three old tires, a rusted metal box spring, and a cannibalized snowmobile. When he couldn't bear to look at it any longer, he turned away. As he walked back to his car, he wished he had never found it. One of the shining memories of his childhood had been turned into a tarnished caricature.

Let's see what The Back Beach has to offer, he thought when he reached his car. Once again, the drive was shorter than he remembered. He and Bran had made this trip on their bikes hundreds of times, and he had made it hundreds more in his head, but here and now, it was like he was making it for the first time. When he reached the beach, and even though he had already seen them on Google Earth, the changes overwhelmed him. Perhaps the biggest shock was the paved parking lot that was completely empty. There were spaces for at least a hundred cars, but not a single one was occupied. On a beautiful day like today, there wasn't a car, or a kid, in sight.

He parked as close to the river as he could, but before walking back to it, he made his way around the expanded sports complex. There was a small playground with slides and a playscape devoid of children. The baseball field was just as deserted, as were the tennis courts and soccer field. It took him a few minutes, but he finally realized why. Even though it was summer, kids didn't wander around on their own these days like he and Bran had. The fear of abductions and perverts would keep them locked away. They were probably all at home on their computers. On weekends, these fields would have been filled with kids playing organized sports. Parents would have lined the sidelines, cheering them on, and the parking lot would be crammed with SUVs and minivans. But today, like most days, it was empty.

When he finally started on the path to what used to be the beach, he was puzzled by the fact that it ran through trees that were way too big. Moss-covered picnic tables were scattered here and there in their shade, but it was obvious they were rarely used. When he reached the water, the mystery of the trees was solved—the area that had been the beach was filled with smaller trees and underbrush. This cleared area was just downstream from where the beach had been. The rock outcropping that Bran had cannonballed him from was now twenty yards upstream. Everything was off just enough to make him feel like a stranger here.

Ryan stood on the shore for ten minutes watching the river flow by. In his mind he could see himself and Bran diving off The Rock on the other side, cannonballing each other and enjoying the river. When the spell broke, he picked up a pebble and tossed it into the water. He turned around and walked back to his car before the current swept the ripples it made downstream. He needed to check in to the Quality Inn he had seen as he got off the highway. The Rock and trestle could wait until tomorrow.

He never saw the reptilian face observing him from the shadows that lined the opposite bank.

Chapter 38

Summer, 1939

Matt and Dave heard the splash the oniare made when it exploded out of the lake, and the larger splash that followed as it disappeared back into the water with Chuck in its grasp. Longo sat there frozen for a few seconds, trying to take it all in, but Matt reacted immediately. He dropped the shotgun into the bottom of the boat, drew his knife, and dove into the water in pursuit of the creature and his brother.

The water was clear enough that Matt could see them ten feet below him. The oniare had Chuck wrapped in a lover's embrace, and it was using its powerful tail to drive them deeper when the rope around Chuck's waist drew taut and brought them to a jarring stop. Matt was still a few feet away when he grabbed the rope and yanked. He couldn't hope to pull them back to him, but he shot toward them like a bullet. When he reached them, the oniare was trying to lock its jaws onto his brother's face.

Matt didn't try to pry them apart. Instead, his slid his

knife between them and drew it across the oniare's throat. He felt it cut through its scales and bite deep into the muscle beneath. In an instant, the creature released Chuck and spun to face him.

As soon as his arms were free, Chuck drew his knife from its sheath and attacked the oniare from behind. As sharp as both knives were, the brothers still had to strain to slice through the creature's scales. While they did, it attacked them with its claws. Within seconds blood filled the water. Chuck was about to plunge his knife into its side for the second time when the rope around his waist yanked him away from the fight and toward the boat. It was Longo trying to save him. He wanted to struggle against the rope to rejoin the fight, but his body was demanding air. Instead, he rose to the surface, gulped in in a quick lungful, and dove under again to rejoin the fight.

Below him, Matt was quickly running out of air, and he was trapped between the oniare and the rope that tethered him to the boat. If he left the fight to reach the surface, the oniare would be free to rip him apart with its claws. Even hampered by the rope around his waist and the resistance of the water, Chuck managed to reach the oniare and plunge his knife into the creature's left eye. Then he quickly withdrew his blade and attacked the right one. The oniare went wild, striking out blindly. Two of the remaining claws on its maimed arm dug into Matt's inner thigh and ripped through skin and muscle, and finally, the femoral artery.

As Matt rose toward the surface, Chuck continued to stab and slash at the creature until he ran out of air. When he left it, the oniare was a blind, bleeding thing no longer capable of fighting back. As soon as his head broke the surface, he filled his lungs with air and plunged back beneath the surface to resume the fight. He had almost reached the monster when his rope brought him up a foot short of his target. He wanted to scream in rage. Instead, he could only watch helplessly as the creature sank out of sight.

"Get in! We need to get Matt to Doc Gordon!" Longo yelled when Chuck's head broke the surface. Chuck was exhausted and his head was swimming from lack of air, but he managed to scramble into the boat without any help.

Matt was lying in the bottom of the boat with a blood-soaked T-shirt wrapped around his leg and Longo's belt cinched as tight as he could get it around his thigh. "Shit," Chuck swore and grabbed the throttle. Within seconds they were skimming across the lake as fast as the motor could propel them.

"Hang on, Matt, we're going to get you to Doc Gordon," Longo told him as he held him in the front of the boat. Matt didn't answer; he had slipped into unconsciousness from the loss of blood. Longo looked up at Chuck and shook his head. "I don't think he's going to make it."

"He will … he has to!" Chuck yelled, and tried to coax a little more speed out of the motor.

When they reached the trestle, Chuck ran the boat right up onto the bank. It skidded to a stop, almost throwing Longo over the bow. "Grab his legs," Chuck yelled as he slid his arms under his brother's shoulders. When they had Matt out of the boat, Chuck threw him over his shoulder and ran toward Longo's car. "You drive," he said as he piled Matt into the back seat.

"Faster!" Chuck called from the back seat. "Go faster!"

"I'm going as fast as I can. If I go any faster over these bumps I'm going to lose it," Longo called back through gritted teeth.

Chuck was going to yell back at him when they hit a

deep rut in the dirt road. The car fishtailed and the rear end clipped a sapling. Longo managed to bring the car out of the skid, straighten it out, and keep driving without slowing at all.

Chuck held his brother's head in his lap, trying to cradle him against the bumping and jarring. "Come on, Matt, hang in there. We'll be there soon, hang on."

When Longo hit the paved road, the ride smoothed out enough for Chuck to feel for a pulse in his brother's neck without risking crushing his throat. He found one, but it was weak, almost nonexistent. "Come on, Matt, hang on," he pleaded.

The car skidded to a stop at Doc Gordon's, and Longo was out of the car and rushing to open the back door to help Chuck get Matt out of the back seat. "I've got him, get Gordon," Chuck snapped at him. He was struggling to get Matt out when he heard Longo pounding on the doctor's door.

"I'm coming, give me a minute," Gordon called from inside. When he finally opened the door, he was shocked to see Longo standing there covered in blood. "Dave, what ..."

Chapter 39

Before he could finish, Longo grabbed his arm and dragged him toward the car. "We have an injured man out here, and he needs you. He's been cut bad, and he's lost a lot of blood."

Gordon came out, saw Chuck covered in blood, and rushed to the car. Then he saw Matt. "My God, what happened?"

Chuck pulled his brother from the car, lifted him in his arms, and started to carry him toward the house. "Later. Just save him."

Doc Gordon looked at Matt and knew there wasn't much hope for the man. "He's lost a lot of blood, and I don't have a supply of blood here. The nearest hospital is a half hour away; he'd never make it that far."

"He's my twin. You can use my blood," Chuck told him.

Gordon didn't want to come right out and tell Chuck his brother was dying, so he said, "Even if I can save him, he's going to lose that leg. The damage is too great and the tourniquet has been on too long."

"I don't care about the leg, just save him."

Gordon knew it was useless, but he couldn't just stand

by and watch the man die, so he agreed to try a transfusion. The most it might do would be to give Turcott's brother a little extra time. Maybe time enough for Chuck to say good-bye.

Chuck was lying on the table, while Matt was on the floor. This would provide the elevation needed to ensure blood flowed from Chuck to his brother. Gordon got the needle in Chuck's arm, started blood flowing through the tube he was using for the transfusion, and placed the second needle in Matt's arm. As the blood flowed, Chuck watched his brother's face for any sign that the transfusion was helping.

Gordon did what he could, but Matt never regained con-sciousness. Chuck grabbed the doctor's wrist when he started to remove the transfusion line. "What are you doing?"

Gordon gently removed Chuck's hand before telling him, "He's gone. There's nothing more we can do for him. But you're going to need some attention, and you can't afford to lose any more blood."

"He can't be gone. Not now. Not after all these years," Chuck moaned, and Longo could hear the desperation in his voice.

"Chuck, I need to take care of you right now."

"Me, why?" Turcott asked.

Gordon pointed to Chuck's torn shirt and the slashes that could be seen through the rips. Some of them were still bleeding.

"I'll be fine," Turcott said as he climbed down off the table and knelt at his brother's side.

"No, you won't. Those wounds could get infected, and some of them are going to need stitches. Now sit there and let me do what I can."

Turcott started to protest until Longo stepped in. "Chuck, let him clean those cuts and stitch them up. Don't let that damn thing kill the both of you."

"Fine," Turcott agreed, "but then we're going back to find that thing."

As Gordon worked on Turcott's cuts, he said to Longo, "More barbed wire, Dave, or are you going to tell me how this really happened?"

"Doc, you wouldn't believe me if I told you, so you're better off thinking it was barbed wire."

"Barbed wire's not going to cut it this time, Dave. I really need to know what happened."

"Go ahead, tell him," Turcott said as Gordon cleaned his wounds.

"Okay, Doc, I'll tell you. There's a ten-foot long creature the Iroquois call an oniare. Legend says it kills and eats people. It has a body like a big snake, but it also has arms. Each arm is tipped by five six-inch claws. Chuck and Matt, that's his brother, were trying to kill it. It did that to them."

"We did kill it," Chuck said from his brother's side.

Gordon stared at them in disbelief, but sensed they were telling the truth. "All right, barbed wire it is," he said as he started to stitch the worst of Chuck's cuts.

* * *

Longo walked into Chief Miller's office and dropped the claw Turcott had given him on Miller's desk. "It's dead."

Miller picked the claw up and turned it over in his hands. "It looks like you're okay. What about Turcott?"

"Chuck's cut up a bit, but he'll heal," Longo answered as he sank into the chair opposite Miller's desk.

Miller could tell there was more to it than that, but he didn't press Longo for the rest of it. He knew Dave would tell him if he just waited.

"Chuck's brother wasn't so lucky. He's dead. The damned thing caught him in the thigh with one of those," Longo said, pointing to the claw. "It opened his femoral artery. He lost too much blood. Gordon couldn't save him."

Miller gave him a puzzled look. "Wait, Turcott has a brother? I never knew that."

"I didn't either, but he did, a twin. It was impossible to tell them apart. He lived down in St. Albans. If he hadn't been with us, Chuck would be dead and the oniare would still be out there."

Miller got up and poured two cups of coffee from the pot in the corner of the room. When he came back, he set one in front of Longo. "So tell me about it. What the hell happened out there?"

Longo took a sip of his coffee before answering. "We were in Cooper Lake when the damn thing launched itself out of the water and grabbed Chuck. One minute he was in the back of the boat working the motor, and the next he was gone. If he hadn't had us tie ourselves to the boat, we never would have gotten him back."

"You tied yourselves to the boat?" Miller asked incredulously.

"Yeah, that was Chuck's idea. Anyway, when we heard the splash and turned around, the oniare had already dragged Chuck into the lake. I was so surprised I just sat there. Matt dove in after them before I even had a chance to think about what to do. He had a hunting knife on his belt; Chuck had one, too, and he went after them with that. When I gathered my wits enough to move, I went to the back of the boat to grab Chuck's rope and try and pull him back." He stopped there to take another sip of his coffee. Miller noticed his hands were trembling when he did.

"I don't know what happened under the water, but when I

got Matt back into the boat, he was bleeding like a stuck pig. I used my belt as a tourniquet, but it wasn't enough. He was cut in other places, too. Chuck wanted to go after the oniare, but we had to get his brother to Doc Gordon, so we let it go. Chuck is pretty sure they killed it, but we're going to go back tomorrow to look for it."

* * *

It took Longo and Turcott two days to find the oniare's corpse. When it sank to the bottom of Cooper Lake, it lay in fifteen feet of water, its snow-white belly just visible from the surface.

Longo held up his hand to Turcott. "Stop the boat. There it is."

Chuck cut the motor back to idle. The boat coasted to a stop ten feet past where Longo had seen the body. Longo directed him as Chuck brought the boat back above the dead oniare, and then he tossed out the anchor to hold them in place.

"Do you think you can get it?" Turcott asked as Longo dropped the grappling hook over the side of the boat.

"I think so. Give me a minute." It took three tries, but Longo finally managed to snag the creature's body. Once he had it, he carefully drew it up. He had to go slowly so the hooks wouldn't rip out. When he had it on the surface, he grabbed it under the arms and muscled it into the boat. They got a good look at what Chuck and his brother had done to it.

Matt's knife had torn through the creature's neck until it scraped along its spine. Chuck's knife had pierced several internal organs as well as both of its eyes.

"What do you want to do with it?" he asked Turcott.

"Burn it. We can do it when we get back."

When they got to the trestle, Longo hauled the oniare from the boat. "Dave, let me help you with that," Turcott offered.

"That's okay, I've got it. Just help me find some dead wood. There should be plenty of it around here."

Turcott nodded his agreement and went off to gather what he could find.

When they had a good sized pile of branches and the broken boards from a few abandoned pallets that someone had dumped near the road, they placed the oniare on the pile. Longo was ready to douse the whole thing with the gasoline Chuck had brought for the boat's motor when Turcott told him to wait. "I want its claws."

Longo stepped back, put the gas can down, and asked, "Why?"

"To honor Matt and to remind me of what he did. Every time I look at them, I'll know we killed a monster."

"You want some help?"

Turcott shook his head, and then took out his brother's knife. He severed each of the creature's remaining eight claws. He placed them on the ground in a neat pile.

"I'd like one of those, if you don't mind," Longo told him when he was done.

Chuck looked down at the claws, selected one, and gave it to Dave. Then he doused the oniare with gasoline, struck a wooden match on his jeans, and tossed it into the pile. It ignited with a loud whoosh and burst of heat.

Neither Longo nor Turcott noticed that the gaping hole in the oniare's chest had not been made by a knife. It had been made by the fetus the creature had never found a host for. Survival would be harder for the young oniare without a host to feed on while it grew, but it was possible. For the next year, the young oniare would hide in Cooper Lake, growing and feasting on anything it could catch. Then it would make its way downriver to Lake Champlain, where it would grow to maturity. It wouldn't return to these waters until it needed a host for *its* young.

Chapter 40

Summer, 1956

Ryan sat at the top of The Rock watching Bran get ready to toss the first stone into the water. He had a hunting arrow nocked and was fidgeting with his bow string. "I really think we should forget about that thing. Let the cops take care of it. They have guns."

Bran brought his arm down and turned to look at him. "We can do this. You've got your bow, and I have this," he told Ryan, waving his father's knife in front of his face.

"Bran, we're just kids. Why do we have to do this?"

Bran lifted his arm to toss the stone, but then brought it down again. "Wait, I almost forgot." He shifted the stone to the other hand and then dug his lucky Indian head nickel out of his pocket and kissed it. Then he shifted the rock back to his right hand. Before he tossed it, he told Ryan, "I'm doing this for my dad. This thing is just like the commies, only it's in our river. We have to fight it."

"But I ..." Ryan started to say, and then the words died

on his lips when he saw the oniare clinging to The Rock below them. It was half out of the water, its claws digging into the granite surface of The Rock.

Bran spun back to the river when he saw the look on Ryan's face. "There it is! Shoot it!"

"It's too far. I need to be closer," Ryan answered.

Bran waved his knife at the creature and then said, "Fine, let's get closer." Then he started down The Rock toward the oniare.

"Wait!" Ryan called. He scrambled after him, stumbled, and dropped the bow and arrow. He managed to grab the bow, but the arrow bounced and slid down The Rock and into the water. Now he only had one left, and it was at the top of The Rock where they had been sitting. "Wait," he called again as he turned back to get it.

Bran heard Ryan call out and saw the arrow bounce past him and into the river, but he kept going anyway. "Come on! Come and get me!" he taunted the oniare as he stayed just out of the creature's reach, trying to draw it out of the water where Ryan would have a better shot at it. The oniare did just that and lunged at him.

"Whoa!" Bran exclaimed and fell backward out of its reach, but not before one of its claws ripped across the left side of his face, slicing it open from cheekbone to chin. The cut wasn't deep, but he felt blood run down his cheek, and it stung like he had been cut with a hot wire.

"Shoot it, shoot it!" he screamed as he crabwalked up The Rock with the creature hissing and clawing its way after him. In his haste to get away from it, he dropped his father's hunting knife, and it followed Ryan's arrow down the face of The Rock. He stared in horror as it bounced into the river. The oniare almost had him when something flew past his head before burying itself into the monster's open mouth.

When the arrow struck, the oniare went wild. Bran continued to crabwalk backward as it struggled with the arrow, trying to grab it and pull it out. It batted at the shaft with its claws, but they were too long and too inflexible to allow the oniare to grasp the slender shaft. All it accomplished was to bat the arrow back and forth, causing the razor-sharp blades of the arrow's head to slice through the soft tissues of its mouth.

"Get up here!" Ryan called from the top of The Rock. All thoughts of attacking the creature with his father's lost knife deserted Bran, and he scrambled back up The Rock to join his friend.

Ryan had dropped his bow and his hands were shaking when Bran reached him. When they looked back at the river, the oniare was gone. "Holy crap! Look at your face," Ryan gasped.

When Bran put his hand up to his cheek, it felt hot and slippery. It had stopped burning, but when he took his hand away, it was covered in blood. He stared at it like he was lost and didn't know what was happening.

It was Ryan who brought him back to his senses. "We have to get you home. You're cut really bad."

"What am I going to tell my mom?" Bran asked as he held his hand against his cheek to stop the bleeding.

Ryan stripped off his T-shirt and handed it to his friend. "Here, use this."

Bran nodded, took it, and held it to his face. "So what are we going to tell my mom? You need to think of something."

"Me? Why me?" Ryan demanded.

"Because you make up better stories than I do."

"That's true," Ryan had to agree. "Your stories are awful."

"We could tell her we were at the dump shooting rats with my slingshot and I fell and hit my face on some broken glass," Bran suggested.

Ryan looked at him like he was crazy. "Are you nuts? We're not allowed at the dump. They have 'No Trespassing' signs all over. We'd be grounded for the summer, and we could get arrested."

"Yeah, right," Bran admitted. "Well, we could …" he started to suggest before Ryan cut him off.

"Will you shut up and let me think?" Ryan snapped. A minute later he thought he had it. "We'll tell her we were catching turtles and you fell and cut yourself on some broken glass."

Bran grinned. "See, I told you, you make up better stories than me. That's a good one."

"Yeah, well, this is it. I'm not going after that thing again. It almost got you this time, and I lost two of my dad's hunting arrows. When he realizes they're gone, I'm really going to get in trouble."

Bran stopped walking and grabbed Ryan's arm. "Wait. My knife. I dropped it. We have to go back. I can't lose it."

"No way," Ryan told him. "We're not going back there. Maybe we can get it after Mister Longo and that other policeman kill the oniare."

Bran started to argue, but the look on Ryan's face told him it would be useless. "You're right, I was stupid. If you hadn't shot that thing, it would have gotten me. Let the cops go after it; they have guns, and it's their job."

"Swear on it," Ryan demanded.

"Cross my heart and hope to die," Bran told him, then spit on his hand and held it out for Ryan to shake.

When they came out of the woods behind Ryan's house, he stashed the bow and the hatchet in the shed before they went in search of Bran's mother. "Let me do the talking," Ryan said. "You just nod and agree."

They found her in the backyard working in her garden. When she saw them, she dropped the cucumber plant she had been ready to put in the ground. "Oh, my God, Brandon, what did you do?"

"We were catching turtles down by the pond. He slipped and fell on a broken bottle," Ryan told her.

"Let me see it," his mother said, reaching for the T-shirt Bran was holding to his cheek. When she tried to pry it away from his face, it stuck to the skin.

"Ow, that hurts," he cried, and snatched it away from her. The movement dislodged part of the T-shirt, and the cut started bleeding again.

"Oh, my God!" she said again. "Get in the car. We're going to the hospital."

Bran pressed the shirt against his cheek and asked, "Can Ryan come?"

"No," she started to say, but then saw the disappointment on Bran's face. "Oh, all right. Ryan, tell your mother where you're going and get back here fast. We're leaving as soon as you're back. And *you*, get in the car," she said, turning back to her son.

Ryan was back in a minute with his mother hustling along behind him trying to keep up. "Helen, is he all right?" she blurted out as Ryan climbed in the back seat with Bran.

"He'll live, but I'm taking him to the hospital in St. Albans to get his face looked at."

"Why the hospital? Why not just go to Doctor Gordon here in town?"

"Because it's his face. I want a surgeon, not some small-town doctor. If he's going to have a scar, I want it to be as inconspicuous as possible."

"Oh, right," Ryan's mom answered as Helen Liotti drove away.

* * *

The drive to the hospital took a half hour. Bran's mom fidgeted as they waited another half-hour before a doctor was able to look at Bran's face. By the time they took Bran into an examination room, she was an emotional wreck.

"Try and hold still," the doctor said as he moistened, and then peeled the T-shirt off the wound. "Hmm," he said when it was off and he could see the entire cut. "It's not too deep, but I think we should stitch it anyway. I'll be as careful as I can. I'll use a lot of small stitches to minimize the scarring. There *will* be a scar, though" he told them. "How did you say this happened?"

"Wait, I want a plastic surgeon to do this," Mrs. Liotti told the doctor.

The doctor stepped away from Bran before answering. "We don't have a plastic surgeon on staff, and it would take hours for one to get here even if we could find one. I think you should let me do this now."

Mrs. Liotti wasn't happy with his answer, but agreed to let him do it.

Since Bran couldn't talk while the doctor was working, Ryan told him what had happened. "We were catching turtles and he slipped and fell on a broken bottle."

"Hmm," the doctor said again as he numbed Bran's cheek with Novocain. "Well, you're lucky it's a clean cut, no jagged edges. It should heal nicely, and the scar shouldn't be too bad. After a year or two, it might fade enough that you won't even see it."

"Oh, thank God," his mom said.

Before he started to stitch the wound, he asked Mrs. Liotti and Ryan to wait in the waiting room. "This is going to take a while, and I don't want any distractions while I'm working. Do you know if he's had a tetanus shot in the last few years?"

"I don't think he's ever had one," Bran's mother answered. "Does he really need it?"

"I think so. I'll clean and disinfect the cut, but it's better to be safe than sorry. Tetanus can be quite serious and very painful."

"Okay," she agreed. Then she and Ryan went to sit in the waiting room. An hour and twenty minutes later, Bran joined them, the left side of his face covered in a white bandage.

"It's numb now, but it's going to sting when the anesthetic starts to wear off. I gave him some codeine and a prescription for more. Only use it if he really needs it, and then only for a day or two. He should stick to soft foods until the stitches come out; I'd say in ten days or so. Bring him back then and I'll look at them. If he's healed all right, I'll take them out then."

When they returned to the car, Bran and Ryan sat in the back. Bran sat on the right so he could lean his head against the window.

"Hey, maybe you'll look like a pirate, just like the ones in the movies. I'll bet Mary Jane Geldart will faint when she sees it," Ryan teased.

"Shut up," Bran answered, but Ryan could see he was smiling at the thought.

* * *

Just before they got back to Poquonock, Bran started wheezing and clawing at his throat. "Can't breathe," he choked out.

"Missus Liotti, Bran can't breathe!" Ryan yelled when he realized his friend wasn't fooling.

Ryan sat in the back seat with his friend, watching Bran's face turn blue and his efforts to breathe get more frantic. He wanted to do something, but there was nothing he could do to help. "Breathe, Bran, breathe," he urged. Bran looked at him, pleading with his eyes for Ryan to do something, anything, to help him. When his eyes glazed over and he slumped in his seat, motionless, Ryan started to cry, sure his friend was dead.

* * *

"What?" Helen Liotti exclaimed, and turned to look back at her son. As soon as she saw him gasping and grabbing at his throat, she hit the brakes and pulled the car over to the side of the street. She started to get out, to run to him, and then realized there was nothing she could do to help him— she had to get him to a doctor. Doctor Gordon was the closest she knew of, so she gunned the motor and sped off toward his office. Mrs. Liotti pulled into Doctor Gordon's driveway, horn blaring. She screeched to a stop, threw open her door, and ran into his office, screaming for help. She reappeared a minute later with Gordon at her heels. He was carrying a hypodermic needle filled with adrenaline. He stuck it in Bran's thigh and pushed the plunger. Then he pulled Bran from the car, laid him on the ground, and started giving him artificial respiration.

He kept at it until Dan Haskell ran over from the volunteer fire department next door with an oxygen bottle and a full face mask. He slipped the mask over Bran's face, tightened the straps, and turned it on. Gordon worked on him for another ten minutes while Ryan watched from the backseat, but in the end, Bran was gone.

Chapter 41

Summer, 2014

Ryan checked into the Quality Inn, got a room on the second floor, and spent the next half hour staring out the window at the mountain—hill, really—that stood between him and Cooper Lake. The only time he and Bran had ever gone there was to go swimming at Echo Rock. The water was clear and deep, and you could jump off the rock shelf next to the rock, but it was a difficult climb back up. The only real attraction the place held was that it was a fifteen-foot leap into the lake, and they could go skinny dipping there. Knowing what he knew now, he would never swim there, nor anywhere else in the river.

Time enough to think about the river tomorrow. Tonight I'm going to have a steak and a beer at Smitty's Tavern ... if it's still there. It was, but not exactly where he expected it to be. He turned off Main Street one corner too soon and was disappointed to find nothing but private homes. When he got to the end, he turned left, went to the next corner, turned left again, and there it was, right where it had always been, just not where he had remembered it.

Ryan knew from the reunion committee's e-mails that some of his old classmates still lived in Poquonock, but he had no real desire to see any of them. Not on this trip anyway. Seeing them could wait until the reunion, when they all came rolling in from wherever they had migrated to over the years. He had no doubt many of them had fled to warmer climes to get away from the Vermont winters.

When he finished dinner, Ryan started to drive back to the Quality Inn, but realized he wasn't in the mood to sit in a motel room and watch television. Instead, he drove to the elementary school and parked in the teacher's lot. Then he locked the car and started walking. He had no idea where he was going until he realized he was following the path he and Bran had taken every day on their way home from school. And, like everything else, the distance between the school and his house was only half of what it should have been. But, he reasoned, his legs were twice as long as they used to be. The entire trip was less than a mile, even though he had to keep to the streets the whole way. Back in the day, he and Bran had cut through four backyards. With the way the streets were laid out, it had trimmed at least half of the distance off their walk.

When he passed the point where Sullivan Avenue had ended in the early days, before the addition of the post-war, four-room crackerbox development houses, the sidewalks ended and he had to walk in the street. Sidewalks had never been part of the development's original plans and had never been added later. They probably never would be. In his day, the streets had been a playground for kids like him and Bran. At this time of night, after dinner, but before darkness, these streets would have been ringing with kids playing hide-n-seek or tag. Now, except for the occasional vehicle, they were empty. One thing hadn't changed, though. There were no fences between any of the houses. The properties just ran together with driveways being the only thing separating them. They were all paved now; when he was a kid, they had just been gravel with compacted dirt underneath.

When he got to the house where he had lived, his mind wandered. He stood in front of it trying to picture what it had looked like back then. The front was unchanged. It was a small Cape Cod with a single picture window on the right side that took up much of the living room wall, a front door with a concrete stoop that was just off center to the right, and another single window on the left. That window marked his parent's bedroom. His bedroom would have been on the same side of the house in the back, but it was smaller because the bathroom was back there, too, between his room and the kitchen. All the rooms had been tiny; his had only fit the bunk beds, the dresser he and his sister had shared, and a small desk. It had been fine for the four of them, but there had been families living in similar houses with three and four kids in them. In those houses, the unfinished attics had been converted into dormered extra rooms that adults could only stand up in at the center.

The house on the left was an exact copy of his old house from the front. Hell, all the houses in the development were. The builders had used one set of plans and popped them out like cars off an assembly line. At least with cars, though, you could order the color you wanted. When they built these homes, you could get any color you wanted as long as it was white. That had changed, though; his old house was now light brown. The one next door was cream.

The house on the right was an entirely different story. If you looked close, you could see the bones of the old Cape showing through, but it had been converted into a two-story colonial with a small porch. The driveway had been widened for two cars, and there was a one-car garage at the end of it. That in itself surprised him. Not one of these houses had a garage when he had lived here. Thinking back, it was hard to remember anyone having two cars. They had had two cars, but only because his dad was a long-haul trucker and gone five days out of seven. He took his car with him to get back and forth from the trucking company he worked for.

After seeing his old house, his mind was in the past as he walked back to the elementary school to get his car. He took a different route this time. On the way, he passed the road to the beach. He stood in front of it for a full five minutes before turning and making his way back to his car. He knew it would be waiting for him in the morning.

Chapter 42

Summer, 1956

Ryan stood outside Blakely's Funeral Home not wanting to go in, but knowing he had to. He was still in a state of shock. Bran was in there lying in a coffin that would soon be closed and taken to the cemetery and buried. After all they had been through with the creature in the river, Bran had died because he was allergic to the tetanus shot the doctor had given him at the hospital. It was like God was playing some kind of cruel joke on them. It wasn't right.

His mother knew he didn't want to go in, but she also knew he'd regret it for a lifetime if he didn't. Knowing Bran was lying in a coffin was bad enough, but seeing him there would be too much. "Come on, Ryan, it's time to say goodbye. You know Brandon would want you to."

Ryan looked up at his mother, nodded, and let himself be led inside on legs that felt like they were stuck in mud. He knew that if he tried to talk, he would start crying. Bran certainly wouldn't want that.

Cold air caressed him like a cool breeze on an autumn day when he went through the doors into the funeral parlor. It was ninety degrees outside … in here it was chilly. He almost bolted back outside when he saw the coffin across a roomful of people standing or sitting in chairs, quietly talking or just staring silently. Bran's mom was in the first row with her back to him, and Ryan dreaded having to talk to her. He was afraid he might slip and tell her how Bran really got the cut on his face. She couldn't know what had actually happened. "Go ahead," his mother said, giving him a gentle push from behind.

Ryan's mind went numb as he made his way to the child-sized coffin where Bran lay. At first, all he could see was its polished wood side, brass handles, and the snow-white satin that lined the inside of the open lid. He almost stopped when the right side of Bran's face started to appear as he got closer. He didn't want to see where the monster had cut him, and the doctor had stitched the gash shut. But he kept walking until he was standing right beside the coffin. At first, Ryan couldn't bring himself to look at his friend's face; instead, he stared at the hands that were folded across his chest. When he finally shifted his gaze upward, it was the bravest thing he'd ever done.

The face was Bran's … and it wasn't. Something was wrong. It was too relaxed, too pale. The stitches and angry slash that should have been running down his left cheek had disappeared, but so had the bright glow of life that had always lit up his friend's face. Bran was gone … really gone. Ryan didn't realize it at the time, but a small piece of him was also gone, and it would never come back. Looking at Bran in that coffin, Ryan realized he wasn't going to live forever. No one was. It was a terrible thing to learn at eleven years old.

He stood for a long time, saying goodbye to the best friend he would ever have. Images of him and Bran playing mumblety-peg, of riding bikes and searching for bottle caps ran through his head. He couldn't even see himself going back to their fort. None of those things would be like they were before without his best friend to share them with. Before he turned to leave, he put his hand into his pocket, took something out, braced himself, and slipped it under Bran's folded hands. They felt cold and waxy, and even though the touch only lasted a second, he would remember it for a lifetime.

When he turned away from the coffin, Mrs. Liotti smiled at him and motioned for him to come over. It was the first time he had seen her move since he had come in. This was the moment Ryan had been dreading. He was the only one who really knew what had happened to Bran, and he couldn't even tell his mother. He couldn't tell her Bran had died trying to kill a monster that lived in the river and killed kids. If he did, everyone would think he was crazy, and no one would believe him anyway. When he reached her, she asked, "Ryan, what did you put in Bran's hand?"

He was both surprised and relieved at her question. "An Indian head nickel. Bran had one—it was his good luck piece."

Mrs. Liotti grasped his hands and said, "I didn't know that. Was that one his?"

"No. His was all worn, and you couldn't even read the date. The one I had was better. I wanted him to have it."

"You both had one?"

"Yeah, but Bran didn't know I had one, too. I only got it because Bran had one, but his was special. He found it in a box in the attic. He said it was his dad's."

"Oh," Mrs. Liotti said before putting her arms around Ryan in a hug. "He loved you very much you know," she told him before letting him go.

"I know," he choked back. The tears Ryan had been holding at bay were ready to break their way out when she asked him another question.

"What happened to his nickel?"

"I don't know. Bran always kept it in that little watch pocket in his dungarees. I know he had it that day, he showed it to me before we ..." Ryan almost said tried to kill the oniare, but he caught himself in time, "... went to catch turtles," he finished.

When he turned to leave, Mrs. Liotti touched his arm one more time. "Thank you for being his friend. I don't know what he would have done without you."

Ryan just nodded and thought, *Yeah, but what am I going to do without him?* Then he walked back through the funeral parlor and went outside where the sun blinded him and the heat hit him like a blow. He felt trapped in the suit jacket his mother had made him wear. When he reflexively shaded his eyes so he could see, Ryan saw Dave Longo. He was there in his police uniform to direct traffic. Ryan flinched when he saw that he was talking to Old Man Turcott. Turcott bowed his head and shambled away looking like a broken man.

When Longo turned and saw Ryan, he waved his hand to call him over. "I'm sorry about Bran. I know how close you two were," Longo told him. When Ryan just nodded, Longo went on. "They say Bran got cut on a bottle, is that right?"

Ryan shifted on his feet before answering, "Yes, sir."

"Ryan, tell me the truth, just between you and me. Was that the way it really happened, or were you two at the river looking for the oniare?"

Ryan was surprised and unsettled by the question. He started to answer, but Longo cut him off. "I need to know because I'm trying to kill that thing. If you were there, you have to tell me where you saw it and what happened. No one else will ever know, I swear."

When Ryan still didn't answer, Longo reached into his pocket and took out the claw from the oniare that he and the Turcott twins had killed in 1939. He held it out for Ryan to see. "I killed one of them a long time ago, and I'm going to kill this one, too. I just need to know where you saw it."

Ryan took a step back when he saw the claw. When Longo saw his reaction to it, he put it back in his pocket. "Well?" he asked.

Ryan nodded. He started slowly by saying, "It was at The Rock," and then the whole story came rushing out. "Bran said we had to kill it for his father. The commies killed his father in Korea, and this was just like a commie trying to kill us. Bran tried to make it come out of the water, and it did, but he slipped and it almost got him. That's when it cut his cheek. It would have gotten him, but I shot it with a hunting arrow and it screamed at us and went back in the river."

"You shot it with a hunting arrow? Where did you hit it?"

"In the mouth. It went right in and stuck in the back of its throat. I don't know how bad I hurt it, but it went away."

Longo was going to say something, but he saw Ryan's mother coming.

"Ryan, it's time to go," she said when she reached them.

Longo stepped back and nodded to her. "I was just telling Ryan I know how hard it is to lose a friend." Then he looked at Ryan. "If you ever need someone to talk to, come see me."

"Okay," Ryan answered, and then he and his mother left for their car. He didn't start crying until they were halfway home.

* * *

The next morning, Mrs. Liotti knocked on their back door. "Is Ryan here?" he heard her ask his mother.

"Yes, come in. I'll call him." She turned to do just that, but Ryan was already there.

Ryan could see she had been crying. Her eyes were dry now, but they were red and her cheeks were blotchy. "I'm going to visit my mother for a while. I'm not sure when I'll be back, but I wanted you to have this before I left. I found it in Bran's dungarees, right where you said it was." When she held out her hand, Ryan saw Bran's lucky nickel. "I think he'd want you to have this."

Ryan reached out, accepted the nickel, and closed his fist around it. "Thank you," was all he could say.

Before things could get too awkward, Mrs. Liotti said, "Well, I really have to go. I'm sure I'll see you when I get back."

Chapter 43

Ryan had been going through his days in a fog since Bran's funeral. He had never felt so alone or guilty. *What if I hadn't dropped that first arrow? What if I had shot it earlier? What if I had refused to go along with his plans to kill it? Would he have gone by himself?*

"I'm going to do it," Ryan said as he sat on the grass in front of Bran's grave, turning his friend's lucky nickel over and over in in hands. "I'm going to kill that thing for you. I don't know how, but I'm going to do it."

* * *

It was a Monday, which meant Ryan's dad was on the road and wouldn't be home for at least three days, but most likely not until Friday. Ryan had to wait until his mom went shopping to sneak into his parent's bedroom and slip the .22 out of the back of his father's closet. He had told Bran that his dad kept it locked up, but that was a lie. The .22 was the one thing in the house that was *really* off limits. If he got caught taking that out of the house, he'd be grounded for life. Now it didn't matter. Life without Bran was like being grounded forever anyway. He didn't know if the .22 would kill the oniare, but if he hit it in the head, it might. He planned on aiming for the spot right between the monster's eyes.

On the top shelf, there was a box of .22 caliber, long rifle bullets that his dad used for hunting squirrels. The box was half empty, which was a good thing. If it had been full, his dad would have noticed any missing bullets. This way he might not notice that some were gone when Ryan put the box back. Ryan stuffed the box in his pocket, grabbed the gun, and took them both to the shed where his mother would never see them. She hadn't been in there since she had seen a large spider in the corner the previous summer.

"What are you going to do today?" his mom asked as they sat at the breakfast table. "I think it's time you got out of the house and did something besides riding your bike to the cemetery. I don't think that's good for you."

"I think I'll go to The Back Beach. Some guys from my class might be there. Maybe I can swim with them."

"That's a good idea. Do you want me to make you a lunch to take with you?"

"Sure," he answered. If she made him a lunch, she wouldn't expect him back before dinner.

"I'm giving you an apple, a peanut butter and jelly sandwich, and a Yoo-hoo. Make sure you bring the bottle opener back," his mom told him as she stood at the kitchen counter making the sandwich. "Do you want anything else?"

How about a hand grenade? he thought, but dared not say it. "No, that sounds good. What are you doing today?"

His mother turned and gave him a funny look. "What am I doing today? Why are you asking?"

"I just want to know, I guess."

"I didn't have any plans. Did you want something?"

"No, I guess not," he answered, trying to look and sound a bit disappointed.

"What?" she asked. "I know you want something."

"Bran was telling me about some guy named Edgar Allan Poe, who writes creepy stuff. He was going to loan me the book, but never gave it to me. His mom's still gone, so I can't get it from her. I was wondering if you could get me a copy from the library."

"I guess I could do that," she said, even though the library was fifteen miles away in the next town. "I'll go over this morning."

"Thanks, Mom," he said. Then he went to his room to put his swimming suit on under his pants.

When Ryan came back, his lunch was ready. It was in a brown paper bag on the kitchen table. "Got your suit and a towel?" his mom asked as he was heading out the door.

"I'm wearing it," he answered, and then showed her the rolled up towel he had taken from the bathroom.

Once outside, Ryan put the lunch and the towel in the basket on his bike and headed toward The Back Beach with no intention of actually going there. His real destination was his and Bran's fort in the woods just behind his house.

* * *

Ryan stood in front of the closed door to the fort trying to build up enough courage to open it. The smell of the damp earth coming from inside triggered too many memories of Bran. When he finally swung the door aside, the fort's cool interior invited him in, but his friend's empty chair mocked him. He pushed it shut when unbidden tears stung his eyes. "Damn you, Bran," he sobbed before walking up the hill toward his back yard. When he got there, he was relieved to see that his mom's car was gone.

Ryan's heart felt like it was going to jump out of his chest, or claw its way out of his throat, as he came down the hill and made his way to the shed. When the dog two houses down started barking, he almost chickened out. Only Bran's lucky nickel in his pocket drove him on. *I'm in my own back yard. Nothing wrong with that. Why am I so nervous?* He knew why, but he couldn't allow himself to admit it—he was scared.

Just get the gun, Ryan thought, but when he opened the shed's door, it was gone. *Oh no … oh no … oh no,* he thought, and started to panic before he remembered he had stood the .22 up behind the rakes and shovels in the back corner. He moved them aside and his hands were shaking when he reached out to grab it. Once he had the rifle and the bullets, he bolted out of the shed and into the woods without even locking the door behind him.

Ryan picked up a few stones along his way to The Rock. He wanted to kill the oniare on the same spot it had cut Bran. When he got there, he stashed the rifle in the woods and went to make sure no one else was there before going back for it. Ryan was in luck. The Rock was deserted.

When he came back and mounted The Rock, he stared at the spot where Bran had been when the creature attacked. Tears stung his eyes. As he wiped them away, he could have sworn he saw Bran looking back up at him. "I wish," he said, and then got down to business.

"Come on, you bastard, come and get me," Ryan said as he tossed the first stone in the water. After five minutes, he was still sitting there waiting, so he chucked another, larger, stone into the river. This one made a bigger splash than the first one had. Ryan sat for another five minutes and still nothing happened. He was ready to throw another stone when he saw something gliding along deep beneath the river's surface. The oniare was definitely here.

Ryan waited for it to come to the surface where he could get a clear shot at it. "Come on. I've got something for you," he coaxed, and smiled when it seemed to be doing just that. But then the creature stopped and hovered a foot below the surface. The oniare's mouth was partially open, but the arrow was gone. It had gotten rid of it somehow. The .22 would be useless if it stayed there.

They remained like that, both waiting, neither moving. *Maybe if I go down, it will come up,* Ryan thought. Before he started down, he picked up the extra bullets he had placed on the rock beside him and put them in his mouth. He would have to eject the spent shell and reload after every shot, and he didn't want to have to try to dig them out of his pockets when he needed them.

Ryan slowly inched his way toward the water by sliding along on his butt, never taking his eyes off the monster. He thought it was also moving, coming closer to the surface, but he couldn't be sure. He stopped when he was still ten feet from the river. Now it was the creature's turn. Any closer and the thing might be able to reach him if it lunged at him like it had at Bran.

Ryan waited … the oniare waited. Neither made any move toward the other. Then, finally, the creature floated up and its head broke the surface. In an instant, Ryan raised the .22, aimed at the spot between its eyes, and pulled the trigger.

"Got ya,'" Ryan yelled and almost choked on the bullets in his mouth when its head jerked backward. His joy was short lived when the monster's gaze returned to him. There was a gash and a bit of skull showing near the top of its head where the bullet had hit it and skidded along the bone. It was the only damage the .22 had done. In the next instant, the oniare lunged out of the water and clawed its way toward him across the rock as he fell backward and fumbled with the bolt in a frantic effort to reload.

* * *

Dave Longo was walking the river, hunting for the oniare by himself. He had a 12 gauge filled with buckshot and was praying he would find it. It had been a week since Bran Liotti's death and the creature was nowhere to be found. Was it possible that Ryan Lowell's arrow had actually killed it? *I doubt it. It's going to take a lot more that an arrow to kill that thing,* he thought. *Matt and Chuck had to damn near cut its head off the last time. No eleven year old is going to kill it with a single arrow.*

Longo was making his way from The Logs to The Rock when he heard the crack of a .22. "Shit!" he swore, and started running.

When Longo burst out of the trees, Ryan Lowell was on his back, trying to reload the rifle in his hands. The oniare was out of the water and clawing its way toward the boy. "Ryan, get back!" he yelled as he ran toward them. There was no way he could use the shotgun with the monster and the boy so close together.

When Longo yelled, the oniare turned its head, giving Ryan just enough time to snap the bolt on the .22 closed and get off a second shot. This one hit the creature on the side of the head. The oniare was stunned, but only for a second. It was going to take more than a .22 slow it down. Ryan was scrambling backward when it lunged toward him again. This time, the boy was well within its reach. "No!" Longo screamed as the oniare reached for Ryan with its claws. Dave had no choice. He had to use the shotgun. He only stopped running long enough to steady his aim. *Oh God, please don't hit the boy,* Longo thought as he pulled the trigger.

The oniare was blown sideways when the shot slammed into it, and a red fog of blood and body parts exploded from it. Longo ran ten steps closer and pumped the slide on the 12 gauge, ejecting the spent shell and jacking another into the chamber. Even with a load of buckshot in it, the oniare was still trying to reach the boy. This time, Longo aimed for the creature's head before pulling the trigger.

Longo's second shot, taken from less than ten feet away, destroyed the oniare's head. Its body flopped back and wound up half in and half out of the water. Its claws were still twitching, scratching on the rock, but Longo was sure it was dead. Now his concerns were for the boy.

"Are you all right? Did I hit you? Did it cut you?" And then, when Ryan shook his head no, "What the hell were you thinking? That's a .22. You couldn't kill a tin can with that thing."

* * *

Ryan looked down at the rifle in his hands. Instead of answering, he shook his head and started to cry. When he looked back up, the oniare was slowly slipping into the river. He still couldn't talk, but he did manage to point at it.

Longo looked where Ryan was pointing and immediately recognized what was happening. "Shit," he swore, and raced to grab it before it could slip off the rock and sink. After all they had done to keep the oniare's existence a secret, he couldn't let it get away only to float down to The Logs. He managed to grab one of its arms and drag it from the river before it was gone. Once he had it out of the water and was sure it wouldn't slip back in, Longo sat next to Ryan to catch his breath and let his heart rate return to normal.

"Is it dead?" Ryan asked.

"Yes, it's dead," Longo answered as they both stared at the creature. It was lying on its back. Even though its snow-white belly was splattered with gore and most of its head was gone, its claws were still twitching.

"Then why's it still moving?" Ryan asked.

"Nerves. A snake will move for hours after it's dead. That thing's just like a big snake."

Longo and Ryan sat together on The Rock and watched the oniare as its claws twitched, sometimes making clicking noises as they knocked together. "Gas," Longo said when its stomach started to ripple and then bulge.

"I don't think so," Ryan said, just before a claw poked through the oniare's gut. Within seconds there was a six-inch slash in the body, allowing a smaller version of the creature to escape its parent's corpse. It was about a foot long and no more than two inches in diameter, but there was no doubt what it was. It hissed at them before fleeing toward the water.

Ryan sat frozen as it tried to escape, but Longo grabbed the shotgun, jumped to his feet, and fired at it before it reached the water. Nothing happened. In the excitement, he hadn't thought to jack a new shell into the chamber. By the time he did, the little oniare had reached the river and was gone.

Chapter 44

Summer, 2014

What the hell? Ryan thought when he pulled into the parking lot at The Back Beach. The lot had always been empty when he had been there before; now there were more than a dozen cars and minivans parked by the ball field. *Aw, shit, it's Saturday. This place is going to be crawling with kids playing baseball and soccer. There's no way I can do what I need to do with them here.*

He thought about going back to the hotel, but it was too nice a day for that. Instead, he took a seat on the bleachers and watched as cars filled the lot, parents filled the bleachers, kids filled the fields, and shouts filled the air. Then two boys arrived on bikes. The first one skidded to a stop and let his drop to the ground. The second glided in, stopped, and carefully placed his on its kickstand. *Me and Bran, back in the day,* he thought. The good feeling he had had sitting there watching the kids turned to cold, black fury. The oniare was in the river—he could feel it. As the boys made their way to the nearest baseball field, he made a promise to himself: *This time, I'm going to kill you, and you're not coming back.*

Ryan had to walk along the soccer field to get to The Logs. From there he intended to walk the path along the river to The Rock, but when he got to The Logs, they were gone and the path to The Rock was overgrown by bushes and small trees. The old road was still there, or at least what used to be the old road; now it was a path not more than a few feet across. *You did this, didn't you? People stay away from the river now, and they probably don't even know why. But those days are over, you son of a bitch.*

As he walked the old road to The Rock, he had the same problem he and Bran had had as kids; over the years it had been picked clean of stones. He managed to find a few along the way; they would have to do.

When he reached The Rock, Ryan stood and stared at it for a minute, imagining what he would see when he climbed to the top. It hadn't looked too different on Google Earth, but his memory had played tricks on him before, so he was prepared for some changes as he made his way up the old familiar steps that were as worn as he remembered them.

I'll be damned—it hasn't changed all that much. The pool in front is a little wider, but that's about it. This would still be a good spot to swim. I'd be tempted to take a dip if I didn't know better, he thought as he looked at the river below.

By now it was ten o'clock; the sun was rising and the granite that made up The Rock was starting to warm up. As he sat at the top, the heat of the day and the stillness of the air lulled him, and for a second he let his mind drift back to the last time he was there. He winced as the vision of the oniare's open mouth flashed across this mind. The blast of Longo's shotgun roared again, like it had in so many of his nightmares. Back then, the sound had deafened him and Longo had sounded like he was whispering even though he was yelling at him, asking if he was all right. And that was the last time he had been at The Rock until today. Then his mind left the past and came back to the present.

* * *

"Are you down there, you son of a bitch?" Ryan said as he tossed his first stone into the river below him. He didn't hold much hope of actually seeing it if it was there, and he couldn't do anything about it if he did, but he wanted to draw it in and let it know he was there. He thought of it as baiting the trap. He'd do the same thing tomorrow. Then, on Monday, when the athletic fields were deserted, and all the parents were back at work and the kids were surfing the net or playing computer games, he'd be back and ready to dance with the devil. As he turned to leave, he saw someone on The Rock, a kid in blue jeans and a white T-shirt like he and Bran used to wear. He started to yell at the kid to get away from the water, but he was only there for an instant, and then he as gone. *That was Bran,* Ryan thought. *He's waiting for me.* On the way back to his car, he convinced himself what he had seen was a figment of his imagination born of the desire to see his old friend once more before he died.

Chapter 45

Summer, 1956

"Aarrgh!" Longo screamed in frustration when he realized the little oniare had escaped. He fired the shotgun into the river in the vain hope that maybe, just maybe, he'd get lucky and hit the damned thing. Then he sat down next to Ryan and put his head in his hands. He knew it was gone, and he felt so useless he wanted to cry, too. He couldn't, though —not with the boy there.

"You want to tell me just what you were thinking to-day?" he asked Ryan when he finally got his emotions under control. Ryan didn't answer, and Longo was going to jump all over him when he noticed the boy was starting to shake all over. *He's in shock,* Longo thought, and put his arm around Ryan to comfort him.

"Ryan, look at it. It's dead."

"Not the little one. It got away."

True, Longo thought, and then remembered the oniare they had killed in 1939. There had been a hole in its stomach, too. *Son of a bitch, that's where this one came from. Am I going to have to do this all over again in seventeen years?* The thought was too much. He couldn't deal with it right now, so he pushed it from his mind and turned his attention to helping the boy.

"No, it didn't," he lied. "My last shot hit it. It was just under the surface. That was buckshot. I saw it get blown a-part in the water. The current carried what was left of it away."

"Are you sure?"

"Oh, yes, I'm sure."

Longo sat next to Ryan until the boy stopped shaking. "I wanted to kill it for Bran," Ryan finally said.

"With a .22?"

"It was all I had. My dad has a shotgun, but I've never used it. I know how to use the .22. I thought if I could hit it in the eye, or right between the eyes, that would kill it."

"You're lucky I was here, you know. That thing would have killed you, and then *your* mother would have been going to *your* funeral."

Ryan hung his head and Longo knew it was starting to sink in. "I know," Ryan answered, so low Longo could barely hear him. "But I hit it. I shot it twice. It moved the first time, but I still hit it in the head. The second time I hit it right in the temple. I know I hurt it."

"Yes, you probably did, and Bran would have been proud, but now it's over. It's dead, and the little one is dead. Now I have to get rid of its body, and you have to forget it."

"I'll never forget it," Ryan told him.

"No, you never will, but you can't tell anyone about it. No one will believe you. They'll just think you're making it up because you're so upset about Bran."

"But, what about ... that?" Ryan said, pointing at the

oniare.

"I'm going to get rid of that. No one will ever know it existed."

"Good," Ryan told him, "because I never want to see it again."

Longo patted Ryan on the shoulder and then made his way to the oniare. He stepped carefully to avoid the blood and bits of the creature's body that lay splattered around it. He tried to grasp it under its arms, but the skin was too slippery. It was like trying to hold a catfish. After it slipped out of his hands the second time, Longo took off his shirt and wrapped it around the body. The shirt was a total loss, but he managed to drag the oniare off the rock and into the bushes.

Then he returned to Ryan. "I'm going to get my car. It's parked at The Logs. When I return, I'm going to load that thing into the trunk and get rid of it. If you're gone when I get back, I'll forget I ever saw you here today." The boy didn't answer; he just nodded to show he understood. "If you ever need to talk to someone about this, come see me, no one else," Longo said before he left.

Longo climbed The Rock, but instead of going back for his car, he slipped into the woods and waited to see if Ryan would actually leave. The boy had seemed like he had gotten over his shock enough to follow directions, but if he had to deal with him and the oniare, it might be impossible to get rid of it without anyone finding out what had happened. He only had to wait five minutes before Ryan appeared. He was carrying the .22 and carefully picking his way down The Rock. When he reached the road, he started running. When the boy was gone, Longo walked back to The Logs, where his car was parked.

Once he was back at The Rock, Longo checked to make

sure it was still deserted before popping the trunk. Everything he needed to get rid of the oniare's body was already in there, but first, he needed to get it back to the car. That's where the body bag came in. Tom Blakely had gotten it for him. The Chief was going to have to replace it, but that was a minor problem.

Once Longo had the body in the bag, and the bag in the trunk, he went about removing all traces of what had happened from The Rock. He used a bucket to rinse the blood and gore from its smooth granite surface, taking particular care to clean all the cracks and crevices. He gathered up the spent shotgun shells and the one .22 caliber casing he could find. The only thing he couldn't erase were the scratches the oniare's claws had made in The Rock's weather-worn surface. They weren't deep, and you had to look really close to see them, but they were there. He thought about trying to scratch them out, but realized that would just draw attention to them. In the end, he left them for Mother Nature to erase with wind and water. It might take years, but she could do it. Let them be a mystery to anyone who might find them.

When all this is done, I'm moving to Arizona. I'm going to live in the desert and not go near another lake or river as long as I live, Longo thought as he drove out of the woods with the oniare in the trunk.

Longo thought about going straight to the station to tell Chief Miller that the oniare was finally dead, but realized he needed to shower and change his clothes before he went anywhere. If he walked in wearing a slime-covered T-shirt and smelling like he did, there'd be questions he wasn't prepared to answer.

When he got to his home, he stripped off his clothes as soon as he was through the door. The T-shirt, undershorts, and pants went into the trash. He would never wear them again. He thought about tossing the shoes, too, but decided he could save those. Then he walked naked through the house on his way to the shower.

He stood under the spray for a full five minutes with the water as hot as he could stand it before he even started to scrub himself with soap and a washcloth. After that, he shampooed his hair three times before the hot water ran out.

When he stepped from the shower, the room was filled with steam and the mirror was covered with condensation. He thought he could still smell the slightest odor of the oniare, and the walls seemed to close in on him. Not caring who might see him, he opened the window wide to air the room out. Then he escaped to his bedroom to towel off and get dressed. He didn't start shaking until he looked at his reflection in the mirror over his dresser. The face staring back at him looked like it had gone through hell.

I need a drink, Longo thought as he sat naked on the bed. He would have had one, too, if there had been one in the house. He knew it was actually the last thing he needed, but *damn,* he wanted one. He wanted to drink until he forgot about the oniare in the trunk of his car, about Brandon Liotti, about Matt Turcott and all the others. He wanted to drink himself into oblivion like he had back in '39. But he had fought and won that battle once. He knew he wouldn't be able to win it a second time. So he sat there until the shaking stopped and he was able to get dressed and face what he had to do next.

* * *

Miller was in his office when Longo came into the station. Erickson and another officer were also there, sitting at their desks. Longo ignored them and went straight into the

Chief's office and shut the door. Then he walked to a chair and sat down without saying a word.

They sat there in uncomfortable silence until Miller finally asked, "What's up, Dave?"

"The oniare's dead. It's outside in the trunk of my car," Longo told him after another period of silence.

Miller was shocked. "It's dead? You killed it by yourself?"

"Yeah." *I had a little help, but you don't need to know that.*

Miller leaned so far back in his chair that Longo thought he might fall ass-over-tea-kettle backward. "Tell me about it," he said.

Longo started to answer and then realized he hadn't thought about the story he was going to tell the Chief. *If you're going to lie, make it as close to the truth as you can,* he thought. "I was at The Rock. I had my shotgun with me. I thought I saw something near the bottom. When I went to get a closer look, the oniare launched itself out of the water at me. I managed to get a shot off. The blast hit it in the head. I wasn't sure if that shot killed it, so I shot it a second time."

"Did anyone else see it—or you with the shotgun?"

"No," he lied. "Then I made sure no one else was around before I put it in a body bag and loaded it into my trunk."

"A body bag? Where the hell did you get a body bag?"

"I had Tom Blakely get it for me," Longo told him.

"When?" Miller wanted to know.

"Right after I knew the oniare was back. Things have changed since '39. Back then we just built a fire and burned the last one. We could never get away with that today. Back then we just piled logs on the bank by the trestle and burned it there. No problem then. Now we'd have people calling in a forest fire and the fire department would be there before the thing was half gone. We need to find another way to get rid of this one. Or, we could just go public now that it's dead."

"I don't think so, not after '39—and not after we've covered it up for this long. We'd have people screaming for our hides. No, we get rid of the thing and forget about it," Miller answered.

Longo knew that arguing was useless. He considered going public with it himself, but that was a bad idea. He'd either be called a liar, or worse, people would believe him and the whole story would come out. That would be bad for him, but worse for Ryan Lowell.

"So how do you want to get rid of it? We have to do it soon. I can't keep the thing in my trunk, and I'm not sticking it in my basement. It'll start to smell."

"We could burn it at the dump. They burn garbage up there all the time," Miller suggested.

Longo shook his head before answering. "Too public. People are always driving up and dropping things off. Plus, Cranston's there." Cranston was the dump man. The town paid him to monitor access to the dump and limit it to town residents. He made sure everything went in the right place and he got his pick of the things people threw away if he thought he could make a buck off them.

"Right, I forgot about him," Miller admitted. "So what the hell are we going to do?"

Longo was about to admit he didn't know either, and then he had an idea. "How about we feed it to John Cranston's hogs?"

Miller looked at him like he was crazy, but then when he thought about it, it actually made sense. The hogs would eat anything, and there were stories about gangsters back in the twenties getting rid of bodies that way. "You think he'd go along with it?" he finally asked.

250

"I don't know, but why tell him? We can drive up at night and just drop the thing in with them. If he finds it, we're the ones he'll call, but from what I hear, John isn't particular about what those hogs eat. That's why none of the locals will buy pork from him," Longo told him.

"So, what, we just drive up there and dump it in their pen?" Miller asked.

"No. If we just dump the entire thing, part of it might still be there in the morning. We need to cut it up and dump it in pieces over a week or two."

"Where are you going to keep it?"

"I'll have Tom keep it in cold storage at the funeral home," Longo told him.

* * *

Tom Blakely was not happy with Longo's solution to getting rid of the oniare. "If you have a better idea, let me know," Dave told him.

"Why not just stick it in a coffin and bury it?" Blakely suggested.

"Think about it, Tom. We'd need a burial plot and someone to dig the grave. And, we'd need to explain who was in the box. You know that," Longo told him.

Blakely had to admit Longo was right. "So let me get this straight. You want me to keep the body here in cold storage, and then you want me to cut it up into pieces so you can feed it to Cranston's hogs?"

"Right."

Blakely shook his head. "I'll keep it here in cold storage in the body bag. I'll give you a key to the back door. You can cut it up and do whatever you want with it. Then give me the key back when it's completely gone. That's as far as I'll go."

"That works," Longo agreed.

Longo's next stop was at Chuck Turcott's.

* * *

Turcott heard the rapping on the front door and decided to ignore it. *Jesus Christ, go away,* he thought as the rapping continued.

"Chuck, I know you're in there. Open the damn door," a voice that could only be Dave Longo called from outside.

It's the oniare. Who'd the damn thing killed now? He dreaded whatever it was Longo had to say, but he knew he had to face it. "What's the damn thing done now?" he demanded when he opened the door.

"Died. It's over at Tom Blakely's in his cold room. I could use some help getting rid of it. You up for that?"

"Damn right. How do you want to do it?"

"Invite me in and I'll tell you the plan," Longo answered.

* * *

Longo parked behind Blakely's Funeral home and he and Turcott made their way to the back doors. Chuck had his knives and Dave had a large galvanized steel bucket with a lid and handles on the sides.

Once they were inside and in the cold room, Longo unzipped the body bag. The smell that came out of it was enough to gag both of them. "You killed it," Chuck said as he took the knife out of the sheath on his belt. "I'll take care of this." Longo couldn't help but notice the name "Matt" burned into the hilt.

"Don't take too much. We don't want any left over for

Cranston to find in the morning," Dave warned him.

"Right," Turcott answered, and cut a twenty-pound piece out of the oniare. Then he cut it into fist-sized pieces that would be easy for the hogs to eat.

Dave cut the lights and parked the car when they were across from the hog pen at Cranston's farm. "You take one handle, and I'll take the other," Longo said as he opened the trunk. "Shit," he swore when the light in the trunk popped on when he opened it. "I forgot about that."

"Don't worry about it," Turcott told him. "There's nobody out here to see us at this time of night."

"Right," Longo agreed, but he planned to remove the bulb before their next trip.

Turcott led the way using a flashlight with a red lens. It threw just enough light to light their path without being bright enough to draw attention from anyone who might drive by on the road. When they got to the hog pen, Longo tipped the bucket over the fence and waited for the hogs to find the meat. They were starting to get nervous when the first one, drawn by the smell, appeared out of the dark. It was followed by three more. Within twenty minutes the meat was gone.

Two weeks later, Dave returned the key. When Blakely checked the spot where the oniare had been, it was empty. Even the body bag was gone. Longo and Turcott had managed to dispose of everything except the claws. They each kept five of them. Turcott placed his in the wooden box that already held his knives and the claws from the one they had killed in '39. Longo smashed his into bits and flushed them down his toilet.

Chapter 46

Summer, 2014

Ryan woke early the next morning. He wasn't hungry, but knew he had to have breakfast. He couldn't let his nerves prevent him from eating. He had to be rested and strong when he finally faced the oniare. Knowing that, he forced himself to wolf down two sausage patties and half a plate of scrambled eggs along with a large glass of orange juice and a cup of coffee at the complimentary breakfast provided by the hotel. It wasn't great, but it definitely filled his stomach.

When he was done, Ryan drove to The Back Beach, stopping along the way once he reached the woods to look for rocks. He stuffed the ones he found into a cloth bag he normally used for groceries back home. It wasn't as easy as he thought it might be. The road was better cared for now and there just weren't that many to be found. After he finally managed to find a dozen or so, he went back to his car and drove the rest of the way to the beach. Then he parked and walked to The Rock.

Here I am again, he thought as he sat on its top, looking down at the river. From where he sat, it looked so peaceful. The current was just enough to carry twigs and leaves along at a pace that could lull a watcher to sleep if they let it. Fish hung almost motionless in the eddy on its right side. He and Bran had tried to catch them back in the day, but they would never bite on anything. It was like they were sunning themselves and going after a worm or lure was just too much work. Leaves that slipped out of the main current into the slack water would circle there in a slow whirlpool until they sank, butted up against the bank, or managed to break free and return to the main flow.

Ryan had timed his arrival to bring him to The Rock at noon, when the sun would be directly above him. There would be fewer shadows on the water then, less sun bouncing off the river at oblique angles that would make it sparkle and shine. It was the best time to look for things that might be hiding in the depths.

He made a careful study of the river, and when he didn't see anything, he tossed his first stone into the water. It hit with a splash. The ripples it made spread out across the surface. He watched as the current deformed them into ovals instead of concentric rings. As they moved, Ryan's eyes scanned the river, looking for any movement under the surface. There was nothing.

He waited five minutes before throwing his second stone. This time, however, he threw two. Each hit with a splash, just seconds apart. He waited, eyes once again scanning the river, and once again, he saw nothing.

He was about to toss another stone when something moved in his peripheral vision. When he turned his head to look at it, it disappeared. *Did I really see something, or was it just a shadow moving across the river? A hawk or turkey vulture?*

He scanned the sky, but, except for a few white, billowing clouds, it was empty. *Come on, you fucker,* he thought, and threw the stone at the spot where he might have seen the movement. It was a further toss than any of the others, and he felt it in his shoulder, a sudden pain that reminded him just how old he was. When the stone hit, something moved under the surface. The skin on his arms and neck prickled as he watched it move upstream, keeping to the shadows near the opposite bank.

There you are, you son of a bitch, Ryan thought. Now that he was sure it was here, he got up, collected his bag of rocks, and walked back to his car knowing that he would return the next day to see this thing to the end. Then, one of them was going to die. He was amazed how calm he felt. This time, he didn't see the young boy standing at the edge of the water.

* * *

Monday morning was overcast with a threat of rain. Not exactly the kind of day Ryan had been hoping for. Rain would make The Rock slippery. He considered waiting for better weather, but he was determined to get this done. If he backed off now, he might not be able to work up the courage go through with his plans. Better to get started as soon as he could and pray the rain would hold off. He wolfed down another quick, complimentary breakfast and was on his way. If everything went as planned, he'd be back for lunch. If it didn't, he wouldn't be coming back at all.

When Ryan got into his car, a calmness filled his being. He was ready for whatever was going to come. He sat there for a moment enjoying the feeling. Then he started the car and drove to The Back Beach. When he got there, he was pleased to find only one car in the parking lot. An old man was sitting behind the wheel drinking coffee and peering out at the overcast sky. He still would have done what he had to do even if the parking lot was full, but this was better.

The rain started as a misty drizzle while he was getting the backpack out of the car's trunk. *Good, that would keep the old guy in his car.* Inside the backpack was the weapon he planned to kill the oniare with: a sawed-off, double-barreled, 12-gauge shotgun. He had sawed off the barrel so it was just over twelve inches in length. He had also cut the stock down so the only part of it that remained was the hand grip. Over-all, the entire thing was less than twenty inches long. This made it maneuverable for close-up work. It would only give him two shots, but all he had to do was pull both triggers to fire them off. He wouldn't have to waste time pumping a new shell into the chamber. He stuck a few extra shells in the pack on the slim chance that he might get to use them. The gun was illegal as hell, but that didn't concern him. He was only going to use it once.

The other thing in the pack was the Kevlar vest he had purchased over the internet. He was counting on it to give him the time he needed to use the shotgun. He'd put that on when he got to The Rock. He didn't want to chance the old man knowing what it was and becoming suspicious enough to call the police. The literature that came with the vest said it was effective against small handguns and knives. It wouldn't protect his arms or neck, but he hoped it would protect him from the oniare's claws for at least as long as it took for him to blow the monster apart. The last thing he grabbed was the bag full of stones. The one thing he didn't have, but now wished he did, was a hat to keep the rain off his head and out of his eyes. Well, there was no help for that, so he slipped the backpack on and headed for his date with the creature that had killed Bran and haunted his dreams ever since.

When Ryan reached the head of the path to The Rock, something half buried in the ground caught his eye. *Damn, is that what I think it is?* he thought as he stooped to pick it up. It was—a Rolling Rock bottle cap. *For luck,* he said to himself as he dug into the small watch-pocket in his jeans to retrieve the Indian Head nickel Bran's mother had given him so long ago. The nickel fit perfectly into the bottle cap. He took it as an omen—and a sign that he wasn't alone. Bran would be with him.

By the time he reached The Rock, the drizzle had turned into a light but steady rain. Small puddles were starting to form in the slight depressions that marred its surface. *It's a good thing I'm wearing boots,* he thought as he started to climb toward the top. He had only taken two steps when he heard the distinctive splash of a stone hitting the water. *Shit, there's someone here! Now what?*

He was still wondering what he would do when he reached the top of The Rock and surveyed the scene below him. There was no one there. His gaze immediately went to the path that led to The Logs before he remembered it was gone, overgrown with saplings and bushes.

What the hell? Someone had thrown a rock, he was sure of that, but there was no one there. It wasn't a fish that had jumped either. The splash had had the *thump* sound that only a heavy stone made when it hit the water. Something weird was going on. The hair on the back of his neck stood on end and goosebumps rose on his forearms. *Nerves,* he told himself, and dug into his bag for a stone.

Ryan's stone hit the water with the same *thump* the mystery one had made a few minutes earlier. The ripples that spread from it mingled with the tiny rings each raindrop made as they struck the river. He tried to peer into the depths, but the surface was like a black mirror reflecting the gray, rain-filled sky above. He wouldn't see the oniare even if it was down there. After the third stone, he dropped the bag, adjusted his Kevlar vest, loaded his shotgun, made sure the safety was off, and started to make his way toward the spot where Bran had been standing when the creature had attacked him. Once he got there, Ryan didn't have to wait long for his enemy.

The oniare exploded out of the water. Ryan had either misjudged where Bran had been when he was attacked, or this oniare was stronger than the last one. Ryan knew it was going to reach him before he could bring the shotgun up and fire it. He felt the creature's arms wrap around him, saw its gaping mouth lunging at his face and smelled its fetid breath. His only hope now was that the Kevlar vest would gain him the few seconds he would need to use the gun. He was trying to bring the gun up to press it against the creature, but the embrace it had him locked in prevented him raising his arm. *I'm going to die,* he thought, and then Bran was there. The terrible gash on his cheek looked worse than Ryan remembered it. As Ryan stared into the open maw of the oniare, Bran raised his arm and drove something into its skull. The monster screamed in pain and released Ryan to claw at a rusted and pitted hunting knife that was now sticking out of the top of its head.

Ryan didn't have time to wonder how Bran had saved him. Instead, he pressed the shotgun to his attacker's chest and pulled the first trigger. The blast blew the oniare back a foot. Then Ryan pulled the second trigger. This shot nearly cut the monster in half. He had won the first half of the battle.

Ryan was breaking and reloading the shotgun when the first claw broke through the creature's stomach. He snapped the gun closed seconds before the head of the little one tore itself free. "Fuck you," Ryan told it as he pulled the trigger. The little oniare exploded in a shower of meat and blood. Ryan didn't wait to see if another one would appear; instead, he stuck the shotgun's barrel into the ruined body of the creature and pulled the second trigger. He reloaded the shotgun and fired into the oniare's body four more times. When he was done, if there had been any more young ones, they were just part of the mass of steaming flesh and spattered gore that remained. Then Ryan picked up the knife that had saved his life out of the pile of offal that had been the oniare. He hadn't seen the knife in fifty-eight years. It was rusted and pitted, not shiny and sharp like it had been then, but he would have recognized it anywhere.

As Ryan turned to go, the rain started in earnest. Before he reached the top of The Rock, it had turned into a hard, cold downpour. There was a flash of lightning, followed almost immediately by a sharp crack of thunder. *That was close,* he thought. When he reached the top, he turned back for one last look at the river. Rivulets of rain were running down The Rock and washing the remains of the oniare into the slowly moving current. *Let it go. I don't care who finds it.* Then a second bolt of lightning lit up the sky, and for a split second, he was sure he saw Bran standing at the bottom of The Rock, looking up at him.

Before he left, Ryan broke the shotgun down into three parts. He flung the barrel into the river and stuffed the rest of it, and the vest, into the backpack. The vest was marked by long tears where the oniare's claws had raked across it. Ryan shuddered thinking about what those claws would have done to his back if he hadn't been wearing the Kevlar.

Ryan's adrenaline rush was wearing off, and he was drenched when he got back to his car. After digging his keys out of his pocket, it took him two tries to hit the correct but-ton to unlock the doors. Once inside, he had to sit and collect himself before he could get the right key in the ignition and start the engine. He let it idle until it warmed enough to turn the heat on. He ran it up to full blast and used it to warm his hands. He didn't put the shift lever into Drive until they stopped shaking.

Ryan was still cold when he got back to the hotel, where he took a long, hot shower. When he was done, he realized he needed two things: food and company. The need for food was natural, the desire for company wasn't. He had never enjoyed loud, noisy, crowded places, but that was exactly what he craved. He needed to be somewhere full of life, of energy—somewhere with people laughing and drinking like the commercials on TV. He hoped the Red Robin across the street would offer that.

It wasn't, but the few customers and quiet ambiance were enough. The Red Sox were on the big screen TV in the bar, and they had Sam Adams Lager on tap. Ryan didn't follow baseball, and wasn't that fond of beer, but he stayed for the whole game, drank at least a pitcher by himself, and ate two chili cheeseburgers and a mountain of steak fries. He didn't leave until closing time. When he walked outside, the rain had finally stopped and a million stars filled the night sky.

* * *

Tuesday morning was the exact opposite of Monday. The sky was clear and a slight breeze rustled the leaves in the trees behind the hotel. After showering and packing, Ryan was ready to go home, but there was still one thing he had to do before he could leave.

It took a while, but he finally found Brandon's headstone

in St. Jude's Cemetery. Like everything else in Poquonock, it wasn't where he thought it would be. "We did it, Bran. You and me. We killed it," he said. Then he knelt down in front of the marker, took the pitted hunting knife out of his pocket, and dug a hole in the grass. He placed the knife, the Rolling Rock bottle cap, and Bran's lucky Indian head nickel in it and carefully covered them over.

Chapter 47

October, 2014

Poquonock High School Class of 1964

Dear Classmates,

The reunion is almost here. We hope you are as excited as we are. We think you'll enjoy all the activities we have planned for you, but the real fun will be seeing old friends and how much Poquonock has changed in fifty years. See you all then.

The Reunion Committee

Ryan closed the e-mail and smiled. He was looking forward to seeing his classmates, especially Betty Hainley. Her name had shown up on the last update, and it appeared she was still single.

ABOUT THE AUTHOR

Dan Foley is the author of the novels "Death's Companion" and "Abandoned," "The Whispers of Crows," a collection of short stories, and the novella, "Intruder." Dan is a New Jersey native who now lives in Connecticut. Before retiring and embarking on his new career as an author, Dan was a licensed Senior Reactor Operator. He taught reactor power plant operations at several nuclear power plants in the U.S. as well as China.

Press
Presents

Stephen McQuiggan's
A Pig's View of Heaven

Twenty years ago, a young woman was murdered, then raped.

A short while later, within the narrow confines of her grave, she gives birth to a child.

Now that child is grown and walking among us – and that can't possibly be a good thing.

Jeffrey Kosh's
Dead Men Tell No Tales

The Caribbean Sea, 1708 AD. In Port Royal, many have heard the legend of the Black Brig, a ship of the damned bringing a fate worse than death to the isolated colonies of the Caribbean Sea. But few know the true story behind the tavern tales. As the war between the Northern Alliance and the League of the Antilles looms on the horizon, an old captain is ready to embark on a venture to cease the blight of the Black Brig once for all and have his revenge. Set in an alternate historical setting, where a supernatural plague caused the fall of the European powers and where what was left of humanity struggles to survive in the New World, *Dead Men Tell No Tales* narrates the ghastly voyage pirate captain Daniel Drake Davies underwent in 1676, and the events that will force him to confront those same horrors thirty years later. For the dead do not rest peacefully in the Devil's Sea. Pirates, voodoo, and seagoing undead await you in this fantastic journey in a land that never was.

Thomas Smith's Monsters

"I killed my parents when I was thirteen years old."

And now, twenty-two years later, after the savagely mutilated body of a pretty young co-ed is found, it's time for Jack Greene to finish what he started.

www.ingramcontent.com/pod-product-compliance
Lightning Source LLC
Chambersburg PA
CBHW071128260626
47162CB00003B/700